# MR. WAS

MR. WHIMSY?

COME ON IN!

*Also by*

**PETE HAUTMAN**

*Blank Confession*

*All-in*

*Rash*

*Invisible*

*Godless*

*Winner of the National Book Award*

*Sweetblood*

*No Limit*

# MR. WAS

PETE HAUTMAN

SIMON & SCHUSTER BFYR
New York London Toronto Sydney New Delhi

SIMON & SCHUSTER BFYR
An imprint of Simon & Schuster Children's Publishing Division
1230 Avenue of the Americas, New York, New York 10020
This book is a work of fiction. Any references to historical events, real people, or real locales are used fictitiously. Other names, characters, places, and incidents are products of the author's imagination, and any resemblance to actual events or locales or persons, living or dead, is entirely coincidental.

For information about special discounts for bulk purchases, please contact Simon & Schuster Special Sales at 1-866-506-1949 or business@simonandschuster.com.
The Simon & Schuster Speakers Bureau can bring authors to your live event. For more information or to book an event, contact the Simon & Schuster Speakers Bureau at 1-866-248-3049 or visit our website at www.simonspeakers.com.
Also available in a SIMON & SCHUSTER BFYR hardcover edition
The text for this book is set in Sabon.
Manufactured in the United States of America
First SIMON & SCHUSTER BFYR paperback edition February 2012
2 4 6 8 10 9 7 5 3 1
The Library of Congress has cataloged the hardcover edition as follows:
Hautman, Pete. 1952—
Mr. Was / Pete Hautman.
1st ed.
216 p. ; 23 cm.
Summary: After his dying grandfather tries to strangle him, Jack Lund discovers a door that leads him fifty years into the past and involves him in events that determine his own future.
ISBN 978-0-689-81068-8 (hc)
[1.Time travel—Fiction. 2. Family problems—Fiction. I. Title.
PZ7.H2887 Mr 1996
[Fic]—dc20
96-11822
ISBN 978-1-4424-3337-3 (pbk)
ISBN 978-1-4391-1574-9 (eBook)

For Smed and Dink

# MR. WAS

## *Author's note*

*In the autumn of 1952, my father was walking the beach along Onslow Bay just north of Wilmington, North Carolina, when he saw something floating in the ocean. Bits of flotsam and jetsam often washed up on the beach, most of it of little value or interest, but when my father saw the silver-colored briefcase bobbing in the surf he waded out into the breakers and retrieved it. I remember the day he brought it home. He had never seen an aluminum briefcase before. They are common today, of course, but in 1952, aluminum was rarely used for anything other than aircraft parts.*

*The briefcase contained four notebooks, which my father, being an inquisitive man, sat down to read. He described the contents of the notebooks as telling a "weird sort of a science fictional story. Something like H. G. Wells, only not nearly so believable." At the time, I had no interest in a bunch of old notebooks, and I never gave them another thought until my father's death in 1991. While going through his things I came across the briefcase in the attic beneath a pile of Christmas decorations. That night I sat down and read the story of Jack Lund.*

*In transcribing and organizing the contents of these notebooks, I have taken a few liberties. Some of what follows is purely speculative, including a few passages describing events of which I have no firsthand knowledge. I truly believe, however, that I have captured the essence of Jack Lund's story. Although at first I read the notebooks as a fantasy, my investigations over the past seven years have convinced me that the events described in Jack's notebooks actually occurred.*

—P. H.

## THE FIRST NOTEBOOK:

# THE DOOR

*This notebook described events occurring early in the subject's life, yet the notebook itself was relatively modern: a cardboard-covered, spiral notebook of the type commonly used by high school and college students in the 1950s. The writing inside was shaky and faint, as if the writer were very old. He used a blue fountain pen.*

*—P. H.*

Andrea Island, Puerto Rico
July 30, 1952

I don't know where to start.

It's not that I don't know what I want to say, but that I don't know what to say first. Andie says I should begin at the beginning, but when was that? Or rather, when will that be? My story is like the surf outside our cottage. Each wave that ends its life on our white sand beach is reborn, again, far out to sea. Is it the same wave? Impossible to say. They are all different; they are all the same.

Andie says to just start telling the story. Andie says it really doesn't matter, as long as it gets told. She says to write until the notebook is full. So I'll begin with the phone call that first brought me to Memory. I was thirteen years old then, but I remember it as if it were yesterday, and that is the way I will tell it.

# Meeting My Grandfather

The ringing woke me up.

I turned my head. The alarm clock's glowing red numbers read 11:59. As the phone rang again, the red numbers changed to 12:00. So that is where we will begin, at midnight, February 17, 1993. It was a long time ago but, as you will see, the memories are still bright and clear.

The phone went silent halfway through the third ring, and I could hear my mother's low voice. I expected her to hang up right away, because a call in the middle of the night was almost certain to be a wrong number, but she didn't. I heard my father grumbling about how was a guy s'posed to get a good night's sleep around this dump. After a few moments I heard my mother hang up.

Everything was quiet for a few seconds, then I heard the shuffling, creaking sounds of someone quietly dressing.

Our rented house, a tiny two-story wooden house in the Chicago suburb of Skokie, was so small you always knew what everybody else was doing. I heard my parents' bedroom door open. A bar of light appeared under my door. I heard footsteps on the tiny landing at the top of the stairs. I could tell by the sound that it was my mother, wearing her regular shoes, not her slippers. My door opened. I saw her framed in front of the brightly lit hallway.

I didn't know what was going on, but I remember getting this feeling in my stomach like something bad had happened.

She walked over to my bed and sat down and put a cool hand on my forehead. Mom always woke me up that way, with the hand on the forehead. I loved the way it felt—soft, firm, and comfortably cool.

"Are you awake, Jack?" she asked.

I nodded, staring up at her silhouette, feeling my forehead move against her palm. She knew I was awake, of course, but she always asked.

"Something has happened." Her voice had a tightness to it, like the sound it had when she was too mad to yell, but this time there was no anger in it. There was something else. "It's your grandfather," she said. "Your grandpa Skoro."

I thought I knew then what she was about to tell me, because I knew that her father, my grandfather Skoro, was getting very old, and his heart was going bad. He lived in a town called Memory, way up in Minnesota, and he was rich. I hadn't seen him since I was a baby. My mother said that since my grandma had disappeared he'd turned into sort of a hermit and didn't like visitors, especially kids. I didn't remember him at all. Every few months Mom would drive up to see him. She said it was to make sure he had enough kipper snacks, rye bread, and corned beef hash. And to give him a chance to yell at her. She would always laugh when she said that.

I had always stayed home with Dad, who also liked to yell at her. While she was gone, Dad and I would eat a lot of pizzas and he would drink a lot of beer. He told me that Skoro didn't care for our sort of company. Once when Dad was in a bad mood from drinking too much he told me, "Your grandfather is a cheap, mean, hard-hearted old miser. Well, he can have his money. I hope he chokes on it." I always remembered that, because when he said it he threw his beer bottle across the room and broke one of Mom's favorite collector plates. He gave me ten dollars to tell her I'd been the one who broke it, and I did, but I think she knew I was lying.

"Your grandfather is dying," my mother said, her voice going all high and funny on that last, final word. Her hand was still on my forehead, but it was no longer cool and comfortable. It had become hot and moist and she was squeezing. I twisted my head away and sat up. She locked both her hands together, pushed them down into her lap, and looked away. The light reflected off tears on her cheek. I didn't like to see her that way.

"Mom? Are you okay?" I asked.

She nodded. "We have to drive up to Rochester," she said. "They have him in the hospital there."

"We? You mean we're all going?"

She shook her head. "Your father's staying here. He's not feeling well."

"You mean he's drunk."

She looked away.

"Why do I have to go?" I asked.

"He wants to see you, Jack. He hasn't seen you since you were a little baby."

"What if I don't want to see him?"

"I need the company, Jack," she said quietly. "Please don't make a fuss." Her eyes were filling up with tears again, so I decided not to argue anymore.

My mother drove as if she expected to be hit any second. When a big semi would blow by us she would duck her head and swerve toward the shoulder. My father refused to ride with her. He said she was a public menace. But Mom wasn't the one whose car was in the body shop every few months. Mom wasn't the one who had tried to drive through the back of the garage. She wasn't the one who'd got drunk and run over the mailbox.

I watched her cringing and ducking and swerving her way out of Skokie, the 1 A.M. traffic zooming by, the defroster in the little Honda rattling, straining to clear the frosted windows. I huddled in the passenger seat, hands inside my down parka, my head scrunched down into the collar like a turtle. After a while, the traffic thinned out and the windows cleared and it got warm enough inside the car so I could relax. I had the feeling that Mom didn't want to talk, but it was pretty boring watching the mileposts flash by.

"I thought Grandpa Skoro didn't like kids," I said.

She flinched, just like she did when Dad yelled at her.

"Now Jack, that's not it at all. It's just . . . he's had a hard time being around people . . . ever since your grandmother . . . left."

My grandmother had disappeared about two years after I was born. Some people said she left on her own, others believed something terrible had happened to her. It was a long time ago. My dad said she was probably dead. My mother didn't like to talk about it.

"So how come he wants to see me now?"

"He's dying, Jack. Maybe he's sorry he never got to know you."

"Well, I'm not."

That hurt her. She drove in silence for a few minutes, then said, "He is a lonely old man."

"Dad says he likes to be alone."

She shook her head. "That's because your father never knew him. They're a lot alike, you know. Angry." She laughed, a high-pitched laugh that I'd never heard from her before.

We didn't talk much after that, and I think I fell asleep.

• • •

My whole life, I've always hated hospitals. When I tell you what happened, and when you get to know more about me, you'll understand. This hospital in Rochester was one of the modern kind where they have colored stripes on the floors so you don't get lost and they try to make things cheery by putting in lots of fake plants in the halls and cheap prints on the walls and the nurses wear bright colors. But it still smelled like a hospital, full of pain and germs and people hooked up to machines.

Grandpa Skoro was hooked up to at least three of them. He had a tube in his nose, another one in his arm, and this thing attached to his chest that led to a complicated-looking video display like you see in the movies with the jagged green line going across a screen.

I could hear my mother suck her breath in when she saw him. He looked like he was dead, but the line on the screen was showing these little blips. His bald, crinkled head was white and powdery-looking, a forest of stiff white hairs shot out from his brow, and his open mouth was rimmed with dried spit. The only part of him that had any color was a long, pink scar running along the line of his jaw. Mom moved in closer, leaned over him, whispered, "Daddy?"

That seemed weird, my mother calling this half-dead old man *Daddy*.

He opened his eyes, pale blue on bloodshot yellow. A grayish tongue crawled across his lips, leaving a glistening layer of spit. He whispered, "Betty."

She pushed her head in past all those tubes and wires and kissed him on the forehead. I stayed back behind her, wishing I was someplace else. I didn't want to get any closer. I was afraid. Afraid of the old man and afraid of the nearness of death. I took a step back, thinking that if I could get out into the hall I could lose myself in the corridors and make my excuses later.

But my mother turned around just then and said, "Jack, come say hello to your grandfather Skoro." She stepped aside so I had a clear view of the old man, and he had a clear view of me.

Grandfather Skoro was smiling, if you could call it that, and reaching out a veiny hand. I started toward him. As I reached his bedside and opened my mouth to say hello, his face changed, as if his flesh were clay in the hands of a mad, invisible sculptor. It began with his mouth falling slack, showing his two remaining peg-like teeth. Then his eyes sort of pushed out of his head and he jerked back away from me like I was a ghost.

"You!" he said, his voice cracking.

I thought, What did I do?

He looked like he was going to die right then and there, but the mad sculptor was not yet done with Skoro. His wide, horrified eyes suddenly went small and glittery. His spiky eyebrows snapped together above his long, twisted nose. His mouth went from round to a bat-shaped snarl, and his pale cheeks bloomed fiery red. I don't remember how he got his hands around my neck, but I remember not being able to breathe, his thumbs sinking deep into my neck, and that face, bright red now from forehead to chin, bearing down on me, my mother screaming, the old man's horrid breath in my face, his wet lips writhing, saying, "Kill you. Kill you. Kill you again."

When I opened my eyes I was flat on my back on the hard linoleum floor, a nurse pressing something cool against my forehead, my mother sobbing hysterically, my grandfather hanging half out of his bed, eyes open and vacant, a bubble of spit frozen on his mouth. The monitor displayed a flat green line, howling its mechanical grief.

# Memory

You'd think that when somebody dies it would be a simple thing to dig a hole in the ground and stick them in it, but I soon found out that life wasn't simple, and neither was death. It was going to take three days to get everything taken care of, three days in Memory, Minnesota, where Skoro had lived his life and where he wanted to be buried.

We left Rochester in midafternoon, drove northeast to Wabasha at the southern tip of Lake Pepin. Lake Pepin is actually a wide spot in the Mississippi, a lake twenty miles long and three miles wide. We followed the shore north. In that part of southeastern Minnesota the river bluffs rise so high you'd almost think you were in the mountains. The road twisted in and out of the narrow valleys, sometimes climbing to the top of the bluffs, then snaking back down to follow the riverbank. Mom drove with her chin pushed forward over the wheel.

"I hate these roads," she said.

We pulled into Memory at four that afternoon. A sign at the edge of town read:

WELCOME TO
MEMORY
POP. ~~47~~ ~~45~~ 40

I said, "I suppose now they'll have to make it thirty-nine."

"I suppose they will," she said dully.

After what had happened back in Rochester it had taken awhile for her to calm down, but she seemed to be fine now. In fact, she seemed more relaxed than I'd ever seen her. Now she was calm, but sad. "You know, when your grandfather was a boy, there were almost a thousand people living here."

"I suppose all the smart ones left," I said.

Mom smiled. She wasn't going to let me get to her. It was as if when Skoro died a huge weight had come off of her.

She said, "When I was your age, there were still about three hundred. It was a good place to grow up. I had a lot of friends." She slowed the car. We were driving past a bunch of old buildings. Most of the windows were boarded up, and the signs were faded and unreadable. "I guess they all decided to leave. Some of their parents still live here."

We came to a traffic light. She brought the car to a stop, even though the light was green.

"They put this stoplight in when I was a little girl. It was supposed to make the tourists slow down so they'd spend their money at the businesses in town. These days there aren't many places left for them to spend it."

"Is everything here closed?"

"There's Ole's bar," she pointed at a low building. OLE'S QUICK STOP was spelled out across the dingy yellow wooden sides of the building in script, the green letters faded and peeling. The two small windows glowed with neon beer signs.

"But that's about it, Jack. The Memory Insurance Company moved their offices to Red Wing, and so did the only bank in town. There was a café up until about five years ago. The co-op is gone. So's the gas station. There's still a little post office, and there's the Memory Institute over there." She pointed at a small, flat-topped wooden building next to the railroad tracks.

"That used to be the depot, but the trains don't stop here

anymore, they just roar on by. Now it's used as a kind of museum."

"Where's Grandpa's house?"

"Up on the bluff. But before we drive up there I'd like to drop in on Orville and Vera Sanders," she said. "I'm sure they'll want to know about your grandfather."

"Do I have to come?" I had an image of sitting around some hot, cramped living room watching a couple of old people drinking coffee.

"What else would you do?"

"I could just walk around," I said. It was a nice day for February, sunny and warm enough to start the snowbanks melting. I figured anything was better than sitting around with Orville and Vera Sanders, whoever they were.

She seemed doubtful, but after a moment she said okay. "Just don't wander too far. I want to get up to the house before it gets dark."

We decided to meet in half an hour in front of the Memory Institute. That's where she dropped me off, telling me that I might want to look at some of the photos. Wouldn't you know, when I tried the door it was locked. A hand-lettered sign on the door said, BACK IN 2 HRS. That was fine with me. Why would I want to look at a bunch of pictures of dead people?

The way the town was laid out, all of the businesses had been clustered on River Street. I walked up the street, looking in the windows of the abandoned buildings. They were either empty, or full of broken furniture and shelving and piles of junk. I turned up one of the side streets. The next street up was called Middle Street. Except for a boarded-up brick schoolhouse, there was nothing but houses. Only about half of the houses had their walks shoveled. The rest looked like they hadn't been lived in for years.

It took me about fifteen minutes to see the whole town,

which was squeezed in between the railroad tracks and the bluff. I didn't see a single one of the thirty-nine people who supposedly lived there, although in some of the houses the curtains seemed to move as I walked past.

I was getting cold. The sun had dropped closer to the horizon and all but disappeared behind a haze of cloud. I headed for Ole's Quick Stop, which turned out to be a sort of grocery store/video rental/bar/café/bait shop. There were two guys sitting at the bar, a couple of identical-looking old men with the dirtiest mesh baseball caps you ever saw, fingers as big around as bratwurst, bellies that looked like they'd had a contest to see who could swallow the biggest medicine ball, butts draping over the stools so far it looked like they'd stuck themselves on the posts. They both turned and looked at me with blank expressions. I didn't get what they were looking at, but I figured I was the only thing they'd seen all day that they hadn't seen a thousand times before. You talk about the boonies, this place was so far out they probably hadn't heard which side won the Civil War.

The guy standing behind the bar—I suppose he was Ole—wasn't much better looking than his customers, but he was younger, he'd shaved more recently, and his cap was newer. You could actually read the embroidered front: WAYNE FEEDS. Who's Wayne? I wondered. I took a look around and saw they had a pinball machine, one of the old-fashioned kind, five balls for a quarter. Half the lights were burned out, but it looked like it would work.

"You got change for a five?" I said to the bartender. He did, and pretty soon I was trying to win games off a machine with a busted flipper and two dead kickers. I had just about got the hang of it when I felt somebody breathing down my neck. I trapped the ball on the flipper and looked back at Ole, if that was really his name, who was standing about two inches behind me, waggling a pair of fuzzy black eyebrows.

"You're pretty good with that," he said.

I shrugged.

"I never seen you around here before. You from out of town?"

I nodded. "I'm just here for a funeral," I said.

That made him step back.

"Who died?" he asked.

"My grandpa Skoro."

His eyebrows went crawling up under the visor of his cap and stayed there. "Old man Skoro?" He turned to the pair at the bar. "You hear that? Skoro didn't make it."

" 'Bout time," one of the men said. The other one snorted a laugh into his beer, sending a gob of foam out onto the bar.

Ole gave me a long look. "You must be Betty's kid."

I nodded.

"So when's the funeral?"

"Day after tomorrow." My finger was getting tired from holding the flipper button pressed. I released the flipper, shot the ball at the nine-ball target, hit it dead on. I got in a couple more flips before the ball drained down the right-hand side. Five hundred ninety-four points.

Ole was still standing there, giving me this look. "So what's gonna happen to Boggs's End?" he asked.

"Huh?" I had no idea what he was talking about.

"Your mom's gonna sell it off, I suppose?"

"I don't know. What's Boggs's End?"

"You never seen the place?"

I shook my head.

Ole laughed. The two guys at the bar just sat there staring at me with their stupid expressions, only now their mouths were maybe open a little farther.

"C'mere, kid," he said, grabbing my arm and starting toward the door.

I thought he was going to kick me out for some reason, so I said, "Hey, I still got games left."

"I just want to show you something. You asked me a question, I want to answer you." He pushed through the door and we walked out into the middle of River Street. A town like Memory, it wasn't necessary to look both ways.

The hazy clouds had solidified into a leaden mass. A few flakes of snow drifted earthward. An icy wind rolled down the bluff and blew into my open jacket. I zipped up and stuck my hands in my pockets.

Ole turned and pointed back over his building at the rock face of the bluff.

"You see it up there, kid?"

I looked where he was pointing. At first, I could see nothing but the sand-colored face of the bluff and the gray clouds above it. Then I saw what he was pointing at. Right at the edge of the bluff, practically hanging from it, perched a huge house almost the exact same color as the clouds.

"What is it?" I asked.

"That's Boggs's End."

"So? What's that got to do with me?"

"You know how come they call it that? On account of it was built by old man Boggs. He lived there with his wife and two daughters, then one day they all disappeared. Poof. Just like that. Back in 1927."

"Really?" I was only mildly interested. I didn't understand what it had to do with me.

"Used to be, people thought it was haunted. You believe in ghosts, kid?"

"No." The longer I looked at that house, the more it looked

to me like a big gray toad. The two small round upstairs windows were the eyes. A strip of smaller windows overlooking the town formed a mouth. A pair of squat turrets, one at each side, were its legs. It looked alive, ready to shoot out its tongue, lapping up people like so many ants. It was such an odd-looking place I wondered why my mother hadn't pointed it out to me.

"Me neither. Anyways, we always called it Boggs's End, on account of it was the end of the Boggses. Even after your granddaddy bought it and moved in back in the forties. Folks still call it that. Specially after your grandma disappeared back in '81."

I said, "That's his *house?*"

"Yep. A hell of a place, ain't it?"

That it was. It was also the place where I would be spending the night. Ole was staring at me with this delighted expression on his face. I looked at his building. The two old guys were standing in the doorway, still giving me that goofy look with their identical mouths hanging open. I thought I knew why my mother hadn't showed it to me. She hadn't wanted to scare me.

# BOGGS'S END

It was snowing hard and getting dark by the time Mom picked me up. After getting that look at "Boggs's End," I hadn't felt like going back into the Quick Stop. I'd been standing in front of the Memory Institute, stamping my feet, trying to stay warm.

"You took long enough," I said when I got in the car.

"I'm sorry, Jack. I had a hard time getting away."

"I coulda froze to death."

I put my hands in front of the heater vents, but the air coming out was still cold. At the north end of town we turned and followed a narrow, winding road up toward the darkening sky. By the time we reached the top the last of the daylight had disappeared. Snowflakes flashed confusingly in the headlights. We were driving into blackness—Mom was hunched over the wheel, pushing her head forward to see better. Trees crowded either side of the roadway, their naked branches dragging against the side of the car. Suddenly, the house appeared in the headlights. Mom stopped the car and we sat staring out through the windshield.

It looked different. Just another big old ugly clapboard house, three stories, with round turrets jutting up from each corner. Not at all like a toad.

Fresh snow coated the circular end of the driveway. All the tree branches and bushes were bent under its weight. Two squat columns supported a wide veranda that sagged in the middle. Our headlights reflected from the dark windows.

"Boggs's End," I whispered.

She nodded, slowly, her eyes tethered to the great gray house squatting before us. Then she gave me a sudden, sharp look. "Where did you hear that?"

"A guy at the Quick Stop."

"Well, don't call it that. I hate that."

We sat in the car in the driveway for what seemed like a long time before Mom opened her door, got out, and shuffled through the snow toward the double front doors.

The first thing we did, once Mom found the right key and got the door open and flipped a light on, was turn up the thermostat, which had been dialed down to fifty-something degrees.

"Your grandfather liked the house cold," my mother said. "When I was a little girl, I was cold all the time."

Then we turned on the downstairs lights, including the huge crystal chandelier in the dining room. You would think turning on about a thousand lights would make a place seem warmer, but it didn't work that way. The rooms were bright, but they were cold, like the inside of a refrigerator. And the air had a stale, lifeless smell. I knew that Grandpa Skoro had died in the hospital thirty miles away, with his hands locked around my neck, but I kept imagining I was smelling his body. Not knowing what else to do, I stood around watching my mother as she worked in the kitchen, throwing out the old food in the refrigerator, washing the crusty dishes in the sink, sweeping up the bits of dirt and old, dried food from the floor. I must've been hanging a little too close, because all of a sudden she turned and said, "Jack, why don't you do something!"

"What?" I said, hoping she wouldn't put me to work scrubbing the floor or something.

"There are six bedrooms upstairs. Pick out where you want

to sleep and dress the bed. The clean linen should be in the closet at the end of the upstairs hallway. And you can take my bag up and put it in the green room." It was her tone of voice where you didn't argue, but just went and did it.

I have to tell you, I didn't feel too comfortable wandering around that house alone. Not like I was worried about ghosts or anything like that. It was just . . . creepy. But I couldn't tell her that, so I grabbed the bags and climbed the wide, C-shaped staircase up to the second floor.

The first bedroom I looked into, the one at the head of the stairs, was yellow. Everything was yellow. The walls were papered with pale yellow-on-yellow flowers, the table by the bed held a bright yellow vase with dead yellow flowers. The lace curtains over the window were the color of dried corn. Even the worn carpeting was a dull, mottled golden yellow. The iron bed, of course, was painted to match. The bare mattress was striped white, beige, and blue, but I was sure there were yellow sheets and a yellow bedspread tucked away in the linen closet.

A painting of a tiger hiding behind a bush hung on the wall above the bed. I stared at the painting for a long time. The tiger looked real, like it was moving, like its eyes were following me. It looked familiar.

The next room down was green the way the first bedroom had been yellow. The wallpaper was dark green fabric with a raised pattern of swirls and twisted teardrop shapes—the sort of shapes I remembered seeing on the insides of my eyelids the last time I had the flu. A bigger room, it had a king-size bed with a mint green canopy, its own private bathroom, and two walk-in closets.

There was also a red room, a brown room, a blue room, and a gray room, the biggest bedroom of all, where Grandpa Skoro had slept. I knew this because the bed was messed up, and his clothes were scattered all over the floor. I closed that door. I didn't want to go in, and I didn't want to look.

And then there was the locked door, which I figured led up to the third floor.

I put my bag in the yellow room, because it was the farthest away from Skoro's bedroom. I found bedding in the linen closet. Every color was available, so I went for blue sheets and a red bedspread—anything to cut down on the yellowness. I didn't think my mom would go for the multicolored look, so I dressed her bed in green.

When I got back downstairs, Mom was heating up a can of corned beef hash. It smelled great. We ate it with saltine crackers, pickles, and shoestring potatoes, which was about all she could find in Skoro's cupboards except for ten cans of kipper snacks, which neither of us liked. A box of vanilla wafers took care of dessert. I was so hungry it didn't even bother me that I was eating a dead man's food.

After dinner I was so tired I could've fallen asleep at the kitchen table. I remember asking Mom why the door to the third floor was locked. She said it was because the house was too big. Grandpa Skoro had kept it closed off to save on the gas bill. Even when she'd been a little girl, she said, they hadn't used that part of the house. Now it was just a big storage space full of broken furniture and junk that was too nice to throw away. She said there were bats up there.

"If you want to look, I'll see if I can find the key," she said. "In the meantime, what do you say we try to get some sleep? You'll have all day tomorrow to look around."

That sounded good to me. I was really tired. Except for sleeping in the car during the ride up from Skokie, I'd been up for two days. And Mom hadn't even had a nap.

"Which room did you pick?" she asked.

"The yellow one."

"That was my room when I was a little girl."

I headed upstairs and fell across the bed. I didn't even get undressed. Sleep came like a giant, soft hand pressing me down into the mattress. In seconds, I was gone.

I sat up in bed. Moonlight filtered through the gold lace curtains. Thinking I was back at home, I wondered why my room looked different. After a second or two, I remembered where I was. And I remembered something else. For a long time, I sat very still, trying to fix the memory in my mind. Then I got up and went to the closet and opened the door.

It reeked of mothballs. I groped for the light, found a cord hanging a few inches in front of my nose, pulled it. The closet was large, about four feet deep and ten feet long. It was empty except for a few clothes hangers hooked over a rod and a mist of spiderwebs filling one corner of the high ceiling. The walls were gray, as was the oddly-shaped door at the far end of the closet. It was shorter than most doors, about five feet high, but of normal width. The knob, tarnished brass with an ornate raised design, was located higher than you would expect. I had a sense of déjà vu, a feeling that I'd been there before, and that I had opened the door.

I reached out, but my fingers hit something solid and invisible a few inches away from the knob. The invisible surface was hard and smooth. I knocked on it, producing a hollow sound. I tried hitting it with my fist. . . .

That woke me up.

I was sitting on the floor in the dark, my knuckles throbbing. Again, I did not know where I was. I stood up, my head hit something, producing a jangly, metallic sound. I ducked and stretched out my hands, felt a wall. I moved along the wall, my heart banging away like crazy. A door. I found the knob, turned it, swung the door open. Faint yellow light. I stepped back into the moonlit bedroom.

I had been in the closet. I must have been sleepwalking, my body acting out the dream.

I turned on the bedside lamp and sat on the edge of the mattress. A few deep breaths later, I started to calm down. As far as I knew, I had never sleepwalked before. I didn't like it. Who knew where I might end up? What if I'd dreamed I could fly? I didn't want to wake up on my way out of the window.

The closet door stood open. I could see the empty wire hangers, one of them still rocking gently.

Might as well have a look, I decided.

The light cord was right where I had dreamed it. I pulled it, and the interior blazed bright yellow. I examined both ends of the closet.

Walls, plain and unadorned.

There was no door.

# The Funeral

The next morning I found my mom sitting in the kitchen drinking black coffee from a fancy china coffee cup. She took a sip, scowled, and set the cup back on its saucer, then saw me standing in the doorway and smiled weakly. "Bitter," she said. "Did you sleep okay?"

I nodded.

A plate of kipper snacks and crackers rested gloomily on the table. She looked at it, shrugged, and laughed. "There's nothing much for breakfast. I don't know how Daddy survived all these years." She took another sip of coffee and made a face. "But I guess he didn't survive in the end, did he?"

It was one of those questions I knew not to answer.

That afternoon, Dad showed up in his beat-up Cadillac with a suitcase full of Mom's and my clothes and a case of beer in a cooler. Or anyway, what was left of a case of beer. He'd managed to drink a lot of it on the drive up from Skokie.

He was in a good mood, but he didn't smile and tell stories and laugh the way he usually did when he was drunk and happy. He was holding it all inside, like he did when he had good news but wasn't ready to tell it. He asked Mom a few questions about the house, and about the funeral arrangements. She answered his questions in a kind of dull, tired voice. I had the feeling she had been glad he'd decided to come up for the funeral, but now that he was here she wished he'd stayed in

Skokie. She kept calling him "Ron, honey," the way she did when he was in a bad mood and she was trying not to set him off.

My father was one of those kind of guys whose face shows everything he's thinking. His mouth was wide and loose when he was happy, or he could tighten it down into a little knot when he was angry. He had thick brown hair like mine, pale brown eyes, and a short, wide nose that sat on top of his bushy mustache. He wasn't a big man—maybe five feet seven inches—but his arms and legs were hard, hairy, and powerful. Sometimes I thought he looked like a gorilla, only not quite as hairy.

My mom was just the opposite—tall, slim, and soft. She had blond hair with just a hint of red when the sun hit it, and deep blue eyes like the sky. I had her eyes, but I had my dad's flat nose.

I told him about how Skoro had tried to strangle me. He laughed. I didn't think it was funny, but I laughed, too, like it hadn't bothered me to almost get killed.

Dad seemed excited about the house. At one point I found him in the dining room, staring up at the chandelier. He grinned at me.

"You know, I bet that old chandelier is worth a few thousand bucks all by itself."

"Really?" It looked sort of ugly to me, but what did I know about chandeliers?

"Old Skoro had a pile of money," he said. "And he never gave us a dime. Well, I guess it was worth the wait."

"So we're going to be rich now?"

He punched my shoulder. "You got it, champ."

Later that afternoon, Mom and Dad drove into Red Wing to meet with the lawyer. I spent about half an hour looking for the TV set before I figured out that there wasn't one. I looked in all the rooms on the first two floors, but the closest thing I could find was the computer in Skoro's study, a PC that must've been ten years old. I turned it on. The monitor buzzed and crackled, then slowly brightened to a dull gray color. A row of five question marks appeared at the center of the screen. Either it was asking me for a disk, or for some sort of code word. I couldn't find any disks, so I tried hitting a few keys at random, but the question marks remained unchanged. After a few minutes I gave up and switched it off.

Skoro had a lot of books in the study, but most of them were pretty boring. Lots of stuff about stocks and bonds and that sort of thing, and a whole shelf full of books about World War II. There were a bunch of old *Reader's Digest*s, and some medical journals, and an album of photographs. I flipped through that. The pictures were black and white. I didn't see anybody I knew. I finally found a book called *An Illustrated History of the American Automobile.* I flipped through the pages, mostly looking at the photos and illustrations. The book was from the 1950s, which meant that the newest, most modern car in it had been built something like thirty years before I was born. I'd never seen most of them, except on old TV movies. After a while I went upstairs to try to get the door to the third floor open.

The lock was the old-fashioned kind with the keyhole shaped like the keyholes in cartoons. My mother hadn't found the key to open up the door to the third floor, so I untwisted a clothes hanger and tried to pick the lock. I'd picked locks before, just for fun, and sometimes it worked. You just have to keep poking around in there. I pushed the end of the coat hanger into the hole and worked it around until I heard something click. Turning the knob, I gave it a pull, but the door still wouldn't budge. I twisted the coat hanger this way and that, working the knob with my other hand, and was about to give it up when I felt something give way. I pulled, and the door swung slowly open, revealing a dusty staircase.

Just then I heard the front door open.

Normally, Mom has a nice voice, deep and clear. But she also has this piercing whine she uses when she's unhappy about something. I couldn't hear what she was saying, but the tone of voice told me that things had not gone well with Skoro's lawyer. I heard my father's deeper voice saying, "It's a load of crap is what it is. How could you not know? He was your father, wasn't he? How could you be so stupid?"

I heard more whining, and decided to go downstairs. Sometimes they would stop fighting when they saw me. Other times I might as well have been invisible. I closed the door, and heard the click of the lock engaging.

By the time I got downstairs they were in the kitchen, my mother sitting in a chair twisting her gloves in her hands, my father cracking open a beer.

"Well, champ," he said, "Your grandfather's screwed us again. He left every last dime to some dump called the Memory Institute."

"That little place in town? I tried to go there but they were closed."

"We still have his house," my mother said, putting on her fake brave smile.

"I'd rather have the two million," Dad said. He took a pull off his beer and left the room. I helped my mom unload the bag of groceries they'd brought back, then watched her make dinner. Pork chops, Dad's favorite, with rice and lima beans, which he hated. Mom would do that sort of thing, and I never understood it. It was as if she played with his anger, like she wanted things to be bad. Everybody thinks their parents are screwed up, but mine should've won some kind of prize.

"We don't have to *live* here, do we?" I asked.

Mom shook her head. "I don't know what we're going to do, Jack."

I found Dad sitting on the living room sofa staring at the wall.

"How's it going, champ?" he said.

I shrugged. "We don't have to *live* here, do we?"

"What, you got a problem with this place?" He laughed, real sarcastic-like.

"It creeps me out," I said. "You know what they call it?"

"What? What's who call what?"

"This place." I swept an arm around the room, taking in all the old-fashioned, beat-up furniture, the heavy, dark brocade wallpaper, the dusty, boring paintings. "The people in town, they all call it Boggs's End."

Dad shook his head disgustedly. "Boggs's End. Wouldn't you know. Not much of a selling point, is it?"

Dinner was quiet. Mom ate with her head bowed, and Dad's jaw kept twitching. He left a pile of lima beans on the table beside his plate. When he had finished eating he took a couple beers with him into Skoro's study. A few minutes later he yelled for me. I found him sitting in front of the computer staring at that row of yellow question marks.

"You know about computers," he said. "How do you work this thing?"

"It's a PC," I said. "I only know Macintosh."

"Well, see what you can do. Kids are supposed to be able to figure this stuff out."

I sat down in front of the computer. "It wants a code word, I think. Five letters or numbers."

"Try his name," Dad said, leaning in over my shoulder. "Type in S-K-O-R-O."

I tried that, then hit the enter key. The disk drive buzzed, the screen flickered, and a line of type appeared on the screen:

OUNDCOMESAROUNDWHATGOESAROUNDCOMESAROUNDWHATG

At first I couldn't read it, then the words snapped into focus. *What goes around comes around.*

"What's that?" My father demanded.

As if in answer, the disk drive squawked and the screen went dark. A curl of smoke rose from the vents on the side of the computer.

"What happened?" my father asked.

"I don't know. I didn't do anything."

"You must have done something! Start it up again."

I tried flicking the on/off switch, but the machine was dead.

My father snorted and said, "Now you've done it, champ."

"I did what you told me."

"Get out of here. Leave me alone."

After that, the only sound in the house was the clinking and scraping sounds of my mother cleaning the kitchen. When she had finished, she sat at the kitchen table with a pen and a book of crossword puzzles.

I tried to read an old newspaper by the light of the chandelier, but I couldn't concentrate. The problem, I realized, was the quiet. There was no traffic or airplane noise, no sound of neighbors' voices, and most of all there was no TV. There wasn't even a radio. This, more than anything, creeped me out. How had old Skoro lived without a TV or radio? I tried to imagine him there, an old man alone, sitting in his living room in the silence. The thought raised the hairs on my arms.

It took a long time to fall asleep that night. The mattress was squishy, the sheets were scratchy, the air in the room tasted cold and stale and dry. I kept hearing strange creaks and pops from the ancient radiators. I hoped that I wouldn't do any more sleepwalking.

As near as I could tell, I didn't.

I didn't get a chance to explore the upstairs the next morning.

"We have to get going as soon as we're done with breakfast," my mom said. "The service is at ten o'clock." She was dressed in a dark blue dress with all her makeup on.

Dad wasn't talking. He looked pale, with a few extra lines on his face. I think he'd sat up drinking beer for most of the night. He hadn't shaved, and his hair was sticking out funny on top. Mom acted casual, like it was no big deal, but she had that tight-eyed look that told me she was holding on to herself. Like if she spilled a drop of coffee on her dress she would start bawling.

I wasn't happy about going to a funeral, but I knew better than to make a fuss. I kind of knew what to expect because my dad's great-aunt Beatrice had died the summer before. Her funeral had been in a big, echoey cathedral that smelled like old wood, candles, and perfume. Most of the two or three dozen people at Aunt Beatrice's funeral had been old ladies. I had asked Mom about that, and she told me that there were always a lot of old ladies at funerals. When I asked her why, she said it was because the men died first.

Later, I found out that that wasn't always true.

Anyways, the part I really hated about that funeral was when I had to look at Aunt Beatrice dead. She'd been sort of ugly when she was alive, and being dead didn't improve her. Her face looked like wax, with some kind of pink stuff rubbed into her cheeks. Her mouth, which I remembered as being a wrinkly, lipless frown, had been turned into a red lipsticked smile. For weeks after her funeral every time I saw an old lady I imagined what she would look like in a coffin, red-lipped and smiling.

Grandpa Skoro's funeral was nothing like that. Instead of being in a big church, it was held at the funeral home in Lake City. The undertaker, a pale old man with a mushy-looking face, took us down the hall to a little chapel. Mom was walking funny, like she had a board strapped to her back, and Dad, who was feeling better after a few cups of coffee, wore the same dreamy, faraway look that he gets when he mows the lawn. The chapel had several rows of hard wooden chairs, some of them occupied. We had to sit in the front row, so I couldn't get a good look at the other people in the chapel without turning around. There were only ten or twelve of them. Mom later told me that Grandpa hadn't had a lot of friends, and those he did have were mostly dead. Dad said something about it looked to him like they were all dead.

The coffin, a huge wooden thing with all kinds of brass hinges and stuff, sat on top of a platform with big vases full of flowers on each side. The top was closed. He had requested a closed coffin funeral and, even though he was dead, he got what he wanted.

The service only lasted about twenty minutes. A tall, thin-faced man with shoulders as wide as a doorway stood up and introduced himself as the reverend such-and-such. He talked for a while, but I didn't hear much he was saying because some guy behind me kept whispering to himself. At first, I thought he was praying, but after a while I started to hear the words. It sounded like he was saying, ". . . around comes around what goes around comes around what goes . . ." over and over, like a chant. I could feel his breath on my neck. It smelled of licorice and dust. I finally couldn't stand it anymore, so I turned around to look at him.

There was no one sitting behind me. The pew was empty.

But I could still hear the words, echoing in my brain: . . . *comes around what goes around comes around what goes around comes around what goes . . .*

Later, at the cemetery, we stood in a little group in the cold snow, everybody wearing long dark coats except me. I had on my red nylon parka with the Chicago Bears logo on the back. I don't know who all the other people were. They all looked old and cold and the same. The mushy-faced undertaker mumbled a final prayer.

We watched them lower Skoro's coffin into a hole in the frozen ground. I asked Dad how they could dig a hole when the ground was hard as rock and he said, "They use coals to warm the ground, then they dig with a backhoe."

The wind blew across the snow and cut up under our clothes. When we finally left, I was shivering. My mom's face was red, and my dad had his chin tucked so far down in his collar that all you could see were his blinking eyes and the white bridge of his nose.

# THE METAL DOOR

Dad came into the kitchen holding his notebook under one arm. He threw it on the counter, grabbed a beer out of the refrigerator, sat down at the table, helped himself to a salami-and-Swiss sandwich, picked up the squeeze bottle of mustard. Dad liked lots of mustard on everything.

"That looks like an old Amish quilt up in the blue bedroom," he said, making a bright yellow mustard scribble on his sandwich.

Mom stood with her back to the sink, watching us. She shook her head.

"Could be worth a lot of money," Dad said, biting into his sandwich. All afternoon he had wandering around the house with a notebook, writing down all the stuff he saw. "We got a key for that third floor?" he asked.

"It's around here somewhere," Mom said. "I haven't found it."

"We don't need it," I said.

They both looked at me.

"I know how to pick the lock," I told them.

Dad laughed. "Studying to be a burglar?" he asked.

"It was just something to do."

He pushed the last of his sandwich into his mouth and stood up. "Let's go check it out, champ. Maybe the old man left us a chest of gold or something."

I caught a look at my mother's face. I couldn't tell if she was mad or ready to cry. I didn't want to know, so I followed my dad up the stairs and went to work with the coat hanger.

This time it only took a few seconds.

"Way to go, champ," he said. "Let's see what we've got."

We climbed the stairs, and it was just like Mom had said. One bedroom was crammed with a bunch of junky old furniture, a trunk stuffed with moth-eaten clothes, and a wooden toolbox containing a bunch of bent nails and a rusty hammer with one broken claw. The other bedroom had nothing in it but a saggy iron bed. I found a yellowed *Life* magazine with Franklin Roosevelt's picture on the cover. We checked all the closets. One of them contained a dried-up dead bat, but we found no chest of gold, no mysterious doors.

Back in the kitchen, my mother was sitting at the table nibbling at a sandwich. Dad grabbed another beer for himself and sat down across from her.

"Just a bunch of junk up there," he said. "All the good stuff is downstairs. I figure an estate sale could net us about nine or ten thousand. We'll have to talk to a realtor about the house and property."

"Ron, he's only been dead three days," Mom said. "Let's not be counting his money so soon, okay?"

Dad glared at her and licked a bit of foam from the corner of his mouth.

I said, "Can we go home pretty soon?"

Mom's shoulders dropped. "First thing in the morning, Jack."

"The sooner the better," Dad said. He tipped his beer and poured half of it down his throat.

Mom said, changing the subject, "It was good to see Mr. and Mrs. Wahl at the funeral. I haven't seen them since I was in college. Mrs. Wahl looks good for her age, don't you think?"

Dad belched. "Which one was she?"

"The elderly woman sitting across from us."

"They were all elderly. I never seen such a collection of walking dead. I thought that one old guy was going to die right there in the chapel. You see him? With the patch on his eye? Who was he?"

Mom shook her head. "I don't know. He looked like he'd been in an accident, didn't he?"

Dad laughed harshly. "He looked like his face met up with a lawn mower is what he looked like."

I didn't know who they were talking about. There had only been a dozen or so people at the funeral, and I hadn't seen anybody with an eye patch or a messed-up face. I asked who they were talking about.

"There was an old man there, Jack," my mom said. "You didn't see him? His face was horribly scarred. He was wearing a black suit."

"I didn't see anybody like that."

My dad said, "Sometimes I think you can't even see the nose in front of your face, champ. The guy was sitting right behind us, talking to himself."

That night they had another fight. I couldn't sleep. My father would start yelling, and then they would both be yelling, and then their voices would lower, and then they'd be quiet for a few minutes, and then Mom's whine would start up and my father would start yelling again. I couldn't understand most of what they were saying, but every now and then I'd catch a few words.

"You want me to leave you? You want us to be poor? Is that what you want? Huh? Is that what you want? Huh? Is that what you want?" One of the things my father would do when he got really mad was to scream the same thing over and over again. I could see the scene in my mind's eye. She would be sitting down, he would be leaning over her, beating her with words.

"Is that what you want? Huh? Is that what you want? Huh? Is that what you want? Huh?"

Her head dropping lower and lower until he stopped, then she would say something and her whine would lash him into a renewed attack.

"You want me to hit you? Huh? Is that what you want? Huh? Is that what you want?"

The argument ebbed and flowed. It had all started over Skoro's house. My father wanted to sell it right away, but Mom wasn't ready to do that. I couldn't figure her out. Why would she want to keep a place like this? I didn't blame Dad for getting mad, but I wished he would quit yelling at her. I thought about going downstairs to see if I could stop it, but I was so mad at both of them myself I was afraid I'd start yelling, too.

After a while, I couldn't take it anymore, so I got dressed, grabbed my blanket, dragged it up to the third floor, spread it out on the old iron bed, and lay down with all my clothes on. The mattress was so saggy my butt nearly hit the floor.

Even with the whole second floor between us, I could hear them. I forced myself to think about things other than my parents. Pretty soon, I was remembering my dream about the door.

Now, I was never one of those people who think that dreams tell us the future. I've dreamed about lots of things that never happened. I've dreamed I could fly, and that I was a dog, and that my mother was made out of cardboard. All kinds of crazy things. But that door dream had me going. I couldn't stop thinking that it was somehow real.

When I'd been up there with my dad I'd sort of rushed from closet to closet, not looking all that carefully. Now I thought I remembered something about one of the closet walls. The more I thought about it, the more I had to look. I rolled off the squishy mattress. Was it the closet in this room, or one of the others?

I opened the door and tugged at the light cord. The old bulb flared yellow. I could see footprints in the dust, from when Dad and I had checked it out earlier. The closet had been empty then, and it was empty now. But I was looking at the end wall. The other walls were plastered smooth and painted gray, but the end wall showed a faint wood grain pattern through its coat of paint. I had seen it before, but I had been looking for a door and it hadn't really registered in my mind. Now, I recognized it as a piece of plywood. I could see the nail heads where it had been hammered into place.

I tried to get my fingers around the edge to pull it loose, but the nails held firm. I would need a pry bar or something. Remembering the tool box we'd found in the other bedroom, I ran across the hall and grabbed the hammer.

When I look back on my life I still have to ask myself whether it is all in my mind. I can see now that I used the door to insulate myself from my parents. In fact, I still wonder if, in some way, I actually created it myself. Was the door real? Am I insane? Did any of this really happen? How do I know I am not sitting in a dark room in a straitjacket staring sightlessly into the convolutions of my own twisted brain?

But then Andie brings me a cup of coffee and a plate of cookies, and rests her cool hand for a moment on the back of my wrinkled neck, and I know that it was real. All of it.

I jammed the one good claw under the edge of the plywood and pried. With a satisfying screech, the nails came loose. The board fell toward me. I stepped back.

Behind the plywood, set a few inches into the wall, was a door. It was not the exact door I had seen in my dream, but it was a door that someone had chosen to conceal.

My heart was going like crazy. I could hear the blood gushing in my ears. Shaking, I grasped the knob. It was cold, and it turned easily. I pulled, but nothing happened. I tried twisting harder, with no result.

Part of me wanted to get out of there. Another part of me could not. To abandon the door would be to go back to listening to my parents, to hear the ugly, muffled sounds of their lousy marriage echoing through the dead halls of my grandfather's home.

I tried pushing. The door swung open with the gritty creak of long unused hinges.

Beyond lay a narrow wooden staircase leading down into darkness. A torn spiderweb, its silken threads dusty and brittle, wafted in the opening. Warm air, soft and stale, swirled over me. I could see by the closet light that the stairway turned to the right after about ten steps.

I started down, still gripping the hammer. I could still hear my parents fighting, but the sound was faint, like poodles barking in the distance.

When I think of myself entering that staircase, without hesitation, without even a flashlight, I wonder what I could have been thinking. What I remember most vividly is the sound of my shoes on the steps, a soft crunching sound, the dried husks of long-dead insects crumbling.

I reached the turn in the stairs. The steps continued down into deeper darkness. I moved down slowly, using the last echoes of light from above to reach the next turn. After ten steps I came to another landing. I stopped. The stairs continued to the left, the blackness below so total that I could see nothing but the little gray spots and squiggles in my own eyes. I had to feel with my feet for each new step, keeping one hand on the wall, one probing the darkness with the hammer, sweeping away the ancient cobwebs, counting each invisible, crunching step.

At the next landing, a faint illumination became visible from below. I could see the bottom of the stairs, and a rectangular shape of some sort. Was it *the* door? The proportions seemed right, but it was hard to see. I took a step, my foot hit something, and suddenly I was falling, my feet in the air. My butt hit the steps and I went sliding painfully down, following the clatter of the hammer and something else, whatever it was that I'd stepped on. For several booming heartbeats I lay crumpled and still at the bottom of the stairs. My butt hurt, and I'd whacked my elbow pretty good, but mostly everything seemed to be okay.

The door was right in front of me, soft green light emanating from its metal surface. Its squat shape was as I remembered from my dream.

I rolled onto my hands and knees and felt for the knob. There it was, high on the door, cold, textured metal, its raised design pressing into the flesh of my fingers. It turned with the same grinding sound I had heard in my dreams. I completely forgot the pain in my rear and my throbbing elbow. A sense of urgency propelled me, as if I knew I had to move quickly before common sense and fear could stop me. I tugged and pushed, but the door remained solid and motionless. Feeling its surface, I discovered a board had been nailed across it. Someone, sometime, had not wanted this door to be found, or to be used.

I felt around on the gritty floor, looking for the hammer. I found the thing I had stepped on first, a little car or something with four metal wheels. No, it wasn't a car. It had leather straps, and it was shaped something like a foot. An old-fashioned roller skate, like kids used to strap onto their shoes. The hammer had tumbled off to the left. I found it leaning against a wall.

It only took a second to rip the board away from the doorway. I grabbed the knob again, and pulled the door open.

Warm, moist, fragrant air flooded over me. I was looking out through a screen of large, dark leaves into a shadowy garden. A greenhouse? There was no greenhouse on the property. I could hear the buzz of insects, and the peeping of tree frogs. What was this place? I pushed the leaves aside for a better look.

If it was a greenhouse, it was bigger than any I'd ever seen or heard of. But if it wasn't a greenhouse, then why wasn't everything covered by three feet of snow? Where had winter gone? The moon, as full and round and bright as it gets, beamed down on what looked like an overgrown field. Was I still in Boggs's End? I forced my way through the vines, stepped out into the knee-high grass. To my right, past the crown of the bluff, I could see a body of water glittering in the distance. I looked back at the doorway, at the vine-covered walls.

It was Boggs's End all right, but it had changed. The paint was flaking off the sides, the windows were boarded up, the grounds were overgrown with weeds, and I knew, without knowing how I knew, that no one was home.

# Scud and Andie

It's difficult to describe the feeling that came over me as I stood staring up at the impossible. I should have been terrified, but I felt no fear stepping through that vine-laden doorway. It was as though I had been pushed too far, as if entering this other world had pushed me beyond shock. What remained was simple wonder.

I was looking at Boggs's End, but it was not the Boggs's End I knew. Where the rows of apple trees had stood was now only a weedy expanse surrounding a collapsed corncrib. The barn was there, but the other sheds were gone.

Had I stepped into the future? If so, how many years had passed? A terrifying thought occurred to me. I looked quickly at my hands, half-expecting to see the wrinkled hands of an old man, but they were as I remembered.

What was this place?

I waded through the grass, circling the house. The moonlight was bright enough to see the cracked windowpanes, the flaking, powdery paint, the rusted steel gutters. Boggs's End looked as though it had been vacant for years. A broken-down tractor with flat tires and vines growing over its engine sat parked in the weed-spotted drive. The tall pine trees that had stood at each corner of Boggs's End were gone, replaced by smaller trees. The front door was sealed with three boards nailed across it. I backed away from the dark house. A jumble of thoughts filled my brain. I wanted to go back through that door, but I also wanted to know where—or when—I was. I started toward the road. The driveway was so overgrown I was sure no one had used it in years.

The road was different, too. The road I recalled was paved, not a rutted, dirt track. I decided to head down the hill, since it was easier than going up. I'd only taken a few steps when I heard a voice.

"Hey, kid."

I stopped and looked around, then saw a figure standing on the other side of the narrow road.

I said, "Who, me?" From his size and the sound of the voice I knew he wasn't an adult, but that only made me a little less scared.

"Yeah. Who d'ya think I'm talking to? Joe Louis?"

"Who's Joe Louis?" I asked.

"The colored boxer. What're you, a dummy?"

I gritted my teeth at that, but let it pass. He stepped forward into the moonlight, showing me a long face with a wide mouth. A strange-looking floppy cap rested atop a pair of large ears. His flannel shirt was rolled up at the sleeves, a pair of baggy bib overalls patched at both knees hung from narrow shoulders. Both hands were buried in his pockets. He was a few inches taller than me, but I guessed him to be about the same age.

"How come I never seen you around?" he said. "You live around here?"

I pointed back at Boggs's End.

He raised his eyebrows, then laughed. "Yeah, sure. Ain't nobody lived there in years, not since the Boggses disappeared."

The Boggses? Boggs was the name of the man who had built the house.

"I bet you run away from someplace, didn't you? I ran away a couple times. One time got all the way to Minneapolis. Where'd you run away from?"

I didn't want to explain, so I just shrugged.

He said, "Well, I guess that's your business. You want to stay in the old Boggs place, I ain't gonna tell nobody. Listen, you hungry?"

"A little."

"Andie and me, we're going to grab some apples off old man Henderson's place. You want to come?"

I said, "Sure. Who's Andie?"

"Kid, you don't know anything, do you?"

"My name's not kid. It's Jack."

"Okay, then. Jack. Let's go, Jack." He started up the road.

I let him get a few yards away, then followed. What else was I going to do? I called after him, "So what's your name?"

He said something over his shoulder. It sounded like "Bud."

I caught up to him. "You say Bud?" I asked.

He shook his head. "Scud. They call me Scud."

"You mean like the missile? Like they were shooting off in Iraq?"

He said, "Rack? What rack?"

I said, "What're you, a dummy?"

He turned toward me, his eyes narrow and his lips pulled back against his teeth. I thought he was going to punch me. We glared at each other for about three seconds. Suddenly his face relaxed and his mouth turned up into a smile.

"Maybe we're both dummies," he said. "What do you say we call it square?"

I nodded and unclenched my fists.

A new voice came out of the night. "Hey, come on, aren't you guys gonna have a fight? Come on, Scuddy-poo. He don't look so big."

I made out the shape of someone sitting on a fence rail, a few yards off the road.

Scud said, "We were just fooling around, Andie. And don't call me that."

Andie hopped off the rail and walked toward us. Dressed like Scud in overalls and flannels, Andie had a long, lanky body, narrow wrists, and an impish, freckled face. It took me a few seconds to figure out that Andie was a girl.

She said, "What's that he's wearin', Scud-doodle? What kind of shoes are those? They're really *strange!*"

Scud hadn't paid much attention to my clothes before, but now he frowned at my Nikes.

"He's got writing all over his shirt," she said. "What's 'Bears'?"

I'd had about enough. I said, "That's a pretty stupid question."

I never saw it coming. Who'd've thought a girl could move so fast? Her sharp fist caught me right in the belly. I staggered back, bent double, trying to catch my breath.

Scud laughed. "Hey, leave him alone, Andie. He don't have any other stuff. He's a runaway. Prob'ly stole off somebody's clothesline. C'mon, let's go."

"Just a second," Andie said. "You okay, Jack-o?"

"My name's Jack," I gasped.

She put a hand on my shoulder. "Hey, I'm sorry I walloped you. You shouldn't a called me stupid."

I stood up straight and looked into her face. I couldn't see what color her eyes were in the moonlight, but they were big and they were looking right at me.

"It's okay," I said. I still couldn't believe that this girl had just knocked the wind out of me.

"You want to come with us?"

I nodded.

About half a mile up the road, the woods opened into a field on the right side. I saw a small, run-down house. A dozen or so small apple trees grew in rows near the back.

Scud said in a low voice, "Keep an eye out, Jack. If he hears us he'll let that dog of his out on us."

"Dog?" I didn't like strange dogs. "What sort of dog?"

"Big," said Scud. "Like a horse."

We eased our way across the ditch and into the orchard. The tree limbs sagged with apples. Scud started right in pulling them off and stuffing them into his shirt. Andie did the same. I grabbed one apple in each hand. My T-shirt wasn't tucked in, so I couldn't put the apples inside it. How many apples were we supposed to be stealing? I turned to ask Scud when suddenly he wound up and hurled an apple at the side of the house. It hit with a bang, exploding into apple bits.

Andie let out a yelp and took off running. Scud laughed and threw another apple. I heard a door open and a howl that turned my insides into jelly. Now Scud was running, too. A black shape—big, like Scud said—rounded the corner of the house with another howl. I took off, bounding across the ditch and into the woods, branches slapping across my face, my heart pounding like a jackhammer. I ran until I couldn't run anymore. Finally I whacked my shin on a log or something and tumbled exhausted into a patch of ferns; I had no idea where I was. I could only hear the air rasping in and out of my lungs. I expected the dog to pounce on me at any second.

Slowly, I got my wind back. The sound of my breathing was replaced by the buzzing of insects. I felt a mosquito on my neck, slapped it, slapped another one that was trying to get into my left ear. I got back to my feet and began to trudge back through the woods, my knee throbbing. I don't know how long I walked, but eventually a road appeared before me. I was about to step out of the trees when I heard an engine. Thinking it might be old man Henderson and his dog, I lay low. Yellow headlights appeared, and a noisy, beat-up antique pickup truck chugged past. I waited until it had disappeared, then went running down the dirt road, hoping to find Scud so I could punch his face in. If I found Andie first, I might even punch her.

The moon had dropped low in the sky, and it was harder to see.

I found Boggs's End before I found Scud or Andie. I had come out of the woods onto the driveway and mistaken it for the road.

I have to explain something here. During the hour or so I'd spent with Scud and Andie, I hadn't thought at all about Boggs's End, or the door, or the fact that in the real world—if that's what it was—snow lay three feet deep over the land. I'd forgotten all of that.

Actually, it wasn't so much that I'd *forgotten*, it was that I had somehow misplaced it in my mind. Seeing Boggs's End standing dark and dim in the fading moonlight brought it all back in a rush.

I wanted to go back.

But would the door work in both directions? Would passing back through that doorway return me to the Memory I remembered?

## Some of the Worst Days of My Life

The door worked both ways. The next morning I woke up to a silent house. I lay staring up at the yellow ceiling, at a strand of cobweb hanging above me.

I asked myself, Is it real?

I remembered climbing the dusty staircase, and the way the fertile scent of summer air gave way to the dry sterility of Boggs's End in winter. I remembered climbing into bed, my mind buzzing with recent memories. I did not remember falling asleep.

My shin hurt.

I pushed aside the covers and found myself still dressed in my jeans and my Chicago Bears T-shirt. An apple, red streaked with gold, perched on the nightstand. I picked it up, felt its roundness, took a bite. Sweet, tart juices flooded my mouth.

It had been real, all right.

Mom was sitting in the kitchen staring down at her empty coffee cup. I poured myself some grapefruit juice and sat down across from her.

"Are we having breakfast?" I asked.

She moved her shoulders up and down about a tenth of an inch. "Make yourself some toast, Jack," A big bruise on her left cheek, another one on her chin.

"Where's Dad?"

"He went back home last night."

"You guys had a big fight, huh?"

"I could make you some eggs, I suppose."

"That's okay. He must've really beat the crap out of you."

"Don't talk like that." Her eyes were wet. "He didn't mean to do it. I made him angry. He feels bad."

"Are we going back home?"

She picked up her coffee cup, swirled the dregs, set it back down.

"What would we do here in Memory, Jack? How would we live?"

I didn't have an answer for that. She peered closely at my scratched-up face.

"What happened to you?"

"Nothing," I said.

Before we left, while Mom was loading up the car, I slogged through the snow to the south side of Boggs's End to look for the door. The vines I remembered were gone, though I could see brown and leafless fragments clinging to the clapboard in places. Instead of vines, there was a snow-covered thicket of some sort. I couldn't see the door. I pushed aside the tangled foliage to get a closer look.

There was definitely no door.

Instead, its squat shape was defined by a patch of siding that did not quite match the original clapboard.

We arrived home in Skokie late. On our answering machine there was a message from a hospital. It turned out that Dad had passed out on the freeway, driven his Cadillac onto the median, across two lanes of opposing traffic, and rolled it in the far ditch. The car was totaled, but Dad survived with only two broken ribs, a mild concussion, a hangover, and an order to appear in court.

After she got over her hysteria, Mom said it was maybe a good thing.

She was almost right.

He was in the hospital for three days. When he got out, on the advice of his lawyer, he started going to the Alcoholics Anonymous meetings at St. Stephen's. The way things changed at home was amazing. It was like he'd become a completely different person. He made it to work every day. He came home every night. We started playing tennis together, and he put up a basketball hoop over the garage. He had lost his driver's license for six months, but when he got it back he bought a Jeep and we went on a fishing trip up in Wisconsin.

Sure, they still had arguments, but they never lasted long. Their fights were about *things,* not about each other. Whatever it was, they would work it out and nobody got hit.

Strangely enough, Dad's new personality seemed to rub off on me. I felt more positive about things, and it seemed to help how I did in school. I started high school thinking that it was going to be really hard, but it wasn't hard at all. I kind of liked it.

The subject of my grandfather Skoro's house rarely came up. The few days we had spent there represented something bad for all of us. I wished Mom would just sell it, but she wouldn't discuss it. She had a job at the mall working at one of the department stores, so she was able to pay the property taxes by herself. Mom would drive up there once every couple months to make sure it hadn't blown over or anything. Dad made it a point not to ride her about it. I think he still felt guilty about his drinking and beating her up. He called it her pet house, but he seemed to tolerate it well enough.

I thought about the door at times, but as the months and years passed the memories seemed more like a dream. Boggs's End could rot away, and that was fine with me. I never wanted to see the place again.

We had two good years.

Sometimes I sit and try to figure out which was the best day of my life. I haven't had a lot of good ones, but some of the best must have been during those years in Skokie when Dad was staying sober. Other times I wonder which was the worst day of my life. There are a lot of choices there, on account of a lot of really rotten things have happened to me, but I keep remembering one day in April, 1995. I was finishing up the tenth grade then, and it seemed like I was growing about an inch a week. I was as tall as Dad, almost as wide in the shoulders, and I could hold my own when we played one-on-one basketball out by the garage. I remember thinking that when he got home from work that day I'd challenge him to a game. I was thinking I might even beat him this time.

But when I opened the door he was home already, sitting on the couch, sort of tilted to the side. At first I thought he was sick.

Then I saw the bottle of vodka propped between his knees.

He was so loaded he could hardly talk. I helped him stand up, and got him upstairs into bed. I went back downstairs and poured out the rest of the vodka. There wasn't much left in the bottle. It smelled like lemons and rubbing alcohol. After that I sat watching TV, the sound turned up loud so I couldn't hear his drunken snores. I don't remember a thing I watched.

When Mom got home I didn't even have to tell her what had happened. She saw the empty bottle by the sink and her face collapsed. I couldn't stand to be there so I went out and wandered up and down the streets of Skokie until long after dark trying to fix my mind on something good. But when the best thing that happens to you all day is that at least your dad got too drunk to beat up your mom, then you know your life sucks. Mostly, that's what I thought about.

Different families handle things in different ways. Dad slept straight through until morning. Breakfast was quiet. It was obvious he was hurting, but we all pretended nothing was wrong. When he left for work, Mom started bawling like I'd never seen before.

We never discussed that night. Without ever talking about it, we somehow agreed to act as if it had never happened. For a couple of months, it seemed to be working. Dad kept right on going to his AA meetings, and after a few suspenseful days Mom lost her haunted, twitchy look and got things more or less back to normal.

Or so we thought.

I couldn't tell you the exact day it began again, because this time he started out slow. What I noticed first was that he had trouble getting himself up and out of the house in the morning. Instead of talking about how he was going to get a promotion, he talked about how he ought to just quit his job. All the people he worked with were jerks, he said. For a while I believed him. But of course, it was my father who was the real jerk.

Mom must've known before I did, because she was sleeping with him. She must've been able to smell it. I didn't get it until I found a couple bottles of peppermint schnapps hidden in the garage.

Before long he was drinking openly and they were fighting again.

Those days are still blurry in my memory, which is just as

well. I spent a lot of nights staying at friends' houses. Dad got fired from his job, of course, and somehow he made it like it was Mom's and my fault.

Things got really bad when he got back on the subject of Boggs's End.

"We had any money I could take my time, find a good job, 'steada living hand t' fist tryin' a make rent every damn month, f'Chrissakes. But no, you gotta be payin' out a fortune on a fallin' down old house in Boondocks, Minne-snow-ta." He kicked one of the kitchen chairs, sent it crashing into the refrigerator.

Mom turtled, pulling inside of herself like a scared snapper. He might as well have been yelling at a rock, which made him even madder.

I was sitting on the living room sofa trying to watch TV, but I could see them through the kitchen doorway, Mom sitting at the table with her shoulders scrunched up, Dad pacing back and forth in his T-shirt and boxer shorts screaming at her. She wouldn't say a word, wouldn't look at him. I figured he would get tired of yelling and go down in the basement where he had his stereo and drink some more and listen to his old Rolling Stones tapes until he passed out. But instead he hit her, his fist ricocheting off the top of her skull. I heard the sound—*tok!*—like a rock hit with a baseball bat, and then a high-pitched moan from my mother.

"Hardheaded bitch," he said, holding his fist, his face contorted with anger and pain.

Mom had her head tucked way down, her arms floating in the air between them, wrists thin and pale, her hands a shapeless and ineffective shield. I held my breath, willing him to turn and walk away.

He grabbed her finger with one hand, bent it back. I heard a snap. He hit her again with his other fist.

I was running at him, shouting. I saw him look up, his eyes red and glittering, and then I was lifted into the air, his hard fist buried deep in my belly, coming up under my rib cage. I landed hard, coughing, barfing my guts out on the linoleum floor. I heard my mother screaming at him. I'll never forget the pattern of those tiles. I heard him grunt with effort, the sound of a blow, then another. Triangles and squares, red and brown, covered with puke. Silence. My father's shoes, walking away. Silence. I turned my head, saw my mother under the table, hugging her knees like a fetus, silent and shaking, red blood spilling from her nose onto her green dress.

Come to think of it, maybe *that* was the worst day of my life. So far.

# Going Back to Boggs's End

One of the neighbors must've called the cops because they came and took Mom to the hospital and my father to jail. Mom had a broken nose and a cut on her forehead and a broken finger. She needed stitches, something like twenty-seven. Except for being a little tender in the belly and not having much appetite, I was okay. I stayed with Mom in the hospital that night. In the morning, the doctor told her she could go home. He told her to take it easy for a few days, but as soon as we got home she started packing. She told me to start packing, too.

"What for?"

"We're going to Memory."

"No way! How come we can't stay here? He's in jail now."

She shook her head. "He'll get out."

It was pitiful watching her try to wrap her knickknacks in newspaper with only one good hand.

"You aren't even going to press charges like the cops said, are you?" I said. "You're going to let him get away with it."

"I just want us to be far away," she said. "Your father has to work out his problem on his own. I can't be a part of it anymore."

I argued some more, but within twenty-four hours I was hauling boxes from a rented U-Haul van through the tall double doors of Boggs's End.

The day we moved was right at the end of July, a few days before my sixteenth birthday.

I did not want to be there.

I did not want to live in that house.

My mother didn't care. All she cared about was getting away from Dad and finding a job. It was a bad time for me, but I think it must have been a worse time for her. Even though she'd grown up there, she didn't really have any friends in Memory. Her friends from school had mostly moved to the city, or to other parts of the country.

Since Mom had refused to press charges, I assumed that my father had been released from jail, but we hadn't heard from him. He must've known where we were. Where else would we go? But he never called. I was both hurt by that, and relieved.

The only good thing was, since there was practically nothing to do in Memory—not a single kid my age—I got to know my mother a little better. At the time, it was no great thrill, but in light of what was to happen, I'm glad we spent that time together.

According to her, Memory hadn't been too much different when she was growing up. More people had lived there then, but the town had been slowly dying ever since the end of World War II. All the kids she'd grown up with in Memory had moved on.

"Daddy was rich," she said, "so all the kids wanted to be friends with me. Only none of them have stayed in touch."

"How'd he get rich?" I asked.

"The stock market. He always seemed to know which companies were going to do well, and he invested in them. As far back as I can remember, he never had to work a day in his life. The people around here, they didn't understand that. I think they thought he was some sort of a criminal. But people liked my mother."

"What was she like?" I asked not because I wanted to know, but because I could see she wanted to talk about it.

Mom let her eyes go out of focus and smiled.

"Feisty," she said after a few seconds. "Nobody pushed her around. You know, Jack, your grandfather could be cruel at times. Mostly he was just mean in the things he'd say, but he would hit you, too, if he was mad about something and you got too close."

"You mean like when he tried to choke me?"

"That was different. He was delirious. But he hit me a few times, I can tell you."

"Like Dad hit you."

She shook her head. "No, not like that. But I saw him go after Mama once. You know what she did? She broke a chair over his head." She laughed. "She was tough. Daddy tried to push her around, but she just wouldn't have it." She paused. "I should have been more like her."

"What do you think happened to her?"

"I don't know. Those later years, after I married your father and we moved to Skokie, I think those were hard years for her. I think she might have just plain run off. I think she must have died somehow, because why else would I never hear from her? The last time I talked to her, we talked about you. You know what the last thing she told me was? She said, 'I'd like to see that boy grow up, Betty dear, I truly would.' That was the very last thing she said to me. But she never did see you grow up. You weren't even two years old. I think if she was alive, she'd have come to see you."

You're probably wondering how come I haven't mentioned the door in the closet.

It wasn't that I didn't think about it. Sometimes I would wake up at night with the sweet taste of stolen apple in my mouth. But I tried to push the memories away. The fact is, I was scared. I was scared that it had been real, and I was scared that maybe it had not.

One night I dreamed I had a dog that could talk. It was no big deal, just a funny dream that I happened to remember, so I mentioned it at breakfast as I was filling the pits in my waffle with maple syrup.

"What did the dog say?" Mom asked.

"I don't know. I think it was some other language. Dog talk. The only word I could understand was 'bubble gum.'"

"Bubble gum?"

"Yeah, isn't that weird?"

She thought it was funny. I liked it when we could start the day off laughing. I was helping her with the breakfast dishes when she asked me if I'd ever dreamed about doors.

I could feel all the little hairs on my neck go straight up.

"What do you mean?" I said.

"Oh, I don't know . . . it's just . . . I used to have dreams about doors when I was your age."

My whole body went tense. I said, "I never dream about doors." Sometimes lies just pop out before I have a chance to think. I didn't want to talk about doors. I could hear my heart pounding in my ears.

"I remember one dream, it was so vivid I thought it was real. You're probably going to think this is funny, Jack. One summer, I was about eight years old, I dreamed that I went through a door in one of the closets upstairs, and I went down a staircase to another door, and I went outside, and it was winter. The air smelled so fresh and clean. It was winter, and everything looked different—the trees, the buildings, everything. I made a snowball and brought it back inside and showed it to Daddy and told him what happened. He took my snowball and threw it in the sink and ran hot water over it until it was gone. He told me I had been dreaming, and I'm sure he was right, but at the time I didn't think so. He finally got me to say I'd only been dreaming, but you know something? I still thought it was real. A few days later, Daddy made me show him the door I'd gone through. I took him to the closet and we looked in and there was no door where I remembered. There was nothing but a wall."

My thumping heart was trying to crawl up my throat. "So you were dreaming?" I asked. My voice cracked, but she didn't seem to notice.

"I suppose I was. The only thing is, I don't remember falling asleep or waking up. Maybe I'm still dreaming. What do you think, Jack? Are you just a part of my dream?"

I shook my head. "I'm real," I said.

But a part of me wondered whether that was true.

That afternoon Mom drove into Lake City to look for a job. I made myself a peanut butter sandwich. We were out of plastic bags, so I wrapped it in a piece of newspaper and stuck it in the side pocket of my jean jacket. I put a can of Coke in my other pocket, then climbed the stairs to the third floor, feeling a little foolish, still half convinced that the door had been nothing but a dream.

# Trying to Buy a Comic Book

I buried my hands in my pockets and faced the wind whipping up the face of the bluff. Below, the town looked like a map, the houses laid out in a grid of gray streets, fading green lawns spotted with red and yellow leaves. Blue smoke corkscrewed up from the chimneys, flavoring the air with the smell of burning wood. The cornfields at the edge of town had gone golden brown, the trees on the skirt of the bluff had lost nearly all their leaves, the sun shone cold and brilliant against a clear blue sky.

I wasn't in August anymore.

Tiny people and black cars moved about the streets. Even from the bluff I could see that all the cars were old-fashioned, like from the thirties. Turning away from the bluff, I rested my eyes on the abandoned hulk of Boggs's End. It, at least, presented a familiar shape.

I had a pretty good idea where I was, but I wasn't quite ready to believe it.

I decided to walk into town. On my way down the winding dirt road I saw only one car. I recognized it as a Model A, just like in *An Illustrated History of the American Automobile,* only this one had been painted bright yellow, and the driver's side door had been lettered in black paint: F. S. DELIVERY. The car slowed and the driver, a blond kid about my age, gaped at me. Another car, an Oldsmobile, came up behind him. The driver beeped his horn. The kid looked back, shifted gears, and continued up the hill.

I was becoming a believer.

The sign at the edge of town pretty much clinched it.

WELCOME TO
MEMORY
POP. 880

Either the town's population had grown by over eight hundred people, or I had been propelled into the past. The closer I got to the center of town, the more certain I became. The streets were paved with smooth brick. Cars and trucks sat casually parked on either side. Most of the vehicles had seen better days. The newest one I saw was a two-tone Buick, brown on gray, probably about a 1940 model.

People stared at me as I walked by. Apparently they didn't get many strangers in town. I walked down to River Street, feeling distinctly self-conscious. The hotel, which had been an abandoned three-story hulk the last time I'd seen it, now sported a fresh coat of white paint. The sign above the lobby door read, NO VACANCY. I looked through the window. Four men sat smoking cigars, staring at a polished wooden cabinet. What were they doing? One of the men reached out and adjusted a knob on the front of the cabinet.

They were listening to an old radio.

Except it wasn't an old radio. It was a new radio.

When was I? I suppose I could've just asked somebody what the date was, but I didn't want to look stupid. I stepped back from the window and looked up the street. No stoplight. The semaphore, I remembered my mom telling me, had been installed when she was a kid. So it was sometime before the fifties, but after the invention of the radio.

The building I knew as Ole's Quick Stop was now called

Gleason's Market. Maybe they would have a newspaper or a magazine. I opened the door and walked in. The woman behind the counter had on the ugliest dress I think I've ever seen, a dull-colored, flowered thing that made her overfed body look even lumpier than it probably was. Behind her, standing on a ladder and wiping the edge of the top shelf with a rag, stood a kid wearing a blue apron over a dingy white sleeveless undershirt and a pair of jeans that hung so low I could see the crack in his butt. His head was separated from his shoulders by a collar of lard-colored flesh. I was staring up at him when the head rotated like that of an owl and his dull brown eyes focused on me. He seemed familiar, as if I'd met him someplace before. I looked back at the magazines, searching for a date.

*Time* magazine. The cover showed a painting of a tough-looking black man. The line under the picture read "Champion Joe Louis." It was the boxer that Scud had mentioned three years ago. I looked for the date on the cover. September 29, 1941.

I had gone back more than fifty years.

Then I saw something that practically stopped my heart. Batman and Robin swinging from thin black lines against a yellow sky, the city horizon red in the background. I read the number in the upper left-hand corner of the comic book

Batman No. 1.

I didn't know much about comic books except to read them now and then, but everybody knows about how the old ones, especially the number one issues, are worth big bucks. Some of them are worth thousands, or even tens of thousands of dollars. The price on the cover said ten cents. Hands shaking, I opened it to the first page.

"Can ah hep yew?"

The woman pressed her belly against the counter and smiled

at me, showing a set of bright yellow teeth, about twice as many as ought to have fit in her head.

"I think so," I said, closing the comic book. "I'd like to buy this, please."

"You from around here?" she asked.

"Just visiting." I dug in my pocket for change.

"That's an old one," said a voice behind me.

I turned and looked into a face identical to that of the kid on the ladder, only this one wasn't wearing an apron. For an instant I thought that the kid had somehow transported himself down from the ladder. I was ready to believe just about anything. But then I saw that the kid on the ladder was still up there. There were two of them, twins.

Suddenly, I knew what they would look like in fifty years. Sitting in this same building, filling their ample guts with beer. The two old guys from Ole's.

"We had the new one, but somebody bought it." I realized he was talking about the comic book.

"Yew shut yer mouth now, Hermie. He wants to buy it. He just said so, din't you, son?"

"That's right," I said, handing her a quarter.

"The Batman, he can't really fly," Hermie said. "Superman is better."

The woman was staring at the coin.

"What's this?" she demanded.

"It's a quarter." Even as I heard the words leave my mouth I realized that I might have a problem here. Did quarters look the same in 1941? The way she was frowning at it, I suspected they didn't.

"Don't look right," she said. She pulled another quarter from a box under the counter and compared the two. "Don't look right at all."

I started to back away.

She squinted at the coin, closing one eye. "Nineteen ninety-three? What are you tryin' to pull on us, boy? This here's a phony!" she hissed.

Hermie snatched the comic out of my hand.

"You stay right there, boy!" The woman shouted at me. She grabbed my jacket sleeve and looked up at the twin on the ladder. "Harry, you get down from there and go get Chief Smaby. You go get him now, boy!"

Harry started down the ladder. I jerked my sleeve out of her grip and took off, hit the door open with my shoulder, and was on the street running when she yelled, "Hermie! Harry! Get him, boys! Get that boy, you go get him now!"

I looked back and saw the twins barreling up the street after me. For a couple of jelly rolls, they could run like crazy. I ran up River Street, ducked down a side street, cut back on Middle Street, and headed for the bluff road. The twins weren't gaining on me, but they still had me in sight and they were yelling, "Stop thief!" even though I hadn't stolen anything. People were opening their doors and looking. The whole town would be after me soon.

I made it to the bluff road, my lungs burning, legs feeling like rubber. A car came rattling up behind me. The only thing to do, I decided, was to head for the trees and try to make my way back to Boggs's End through the woods. I hit the ditch running, then heard a voice shouting, "Hey! You need a lift?"

I stopped and looked back at the car. It was the same yellow Model A that had passed me on the way down. The blond kid was leaning out the window, grinning. "What you runnin' from?" he asked.

Now that I could see him better, I recognized that long, narrow face with the wide mouth. "Scud?"

He flexed his brow. "You know me?"

I looked back down the hill, breathing hard. "I'm Jack. You remember me?"

His eyes widened. "You still runnin' from that dog?" He laughed.

The twins were coming around the bend, followed by a man in overalls and, farther back, the fat woman from the store. I ran to the car and hopped in. "Let's go!"

Scud revved up the engine and popped the clutch. The tires gave a squeak and we started up the hill, slowly picking up speed.

"What'd you do, rob 'em or something?"

"I tried to buy a comic book," I panted, trying to catch my breath.

He looked back down the road. "That's a lot of runnin' for one comic book."

I sat back. "You can say that again."

"So what did you do? Try to swipe it?"

"Something like that."

Scud laughed. "So where you been? Me and Andie, we only seen you that one night, what, two or three years ago?"

"I've been busy."

"Doin' what? Where you from, anyways?"

I hesitated, wondering whether I should tell him, thinking he probably wouldn't believe me if I did. Scud was helping me out of my current predicament, but I had no reason to trust him, especially after his stunt in the apple orchard. Of course, a kid can change a lot in three years. We were both older and, I hoped, smarter. But I decided to play it safe.

"I was just passing through," I said.

"What, you run away again or something?"

"Yeah."

"You need a place to stay?"

"Nah."

"So where you want to go?"

We were coming up on the driveway leading to Boggs's End. "You let me out here," I said.

"Here? Why? You want 'em to catch you? They ain't but a mile back. Old Mrs. Gleason, she's mad enough she'll run all night. And Harry and Hermie, they won't stop till she tells 'em." He laughed.

We passed the driveway, still picking up speed.

Scud said, "What do you say we drop in on Andie? She'll be tickled to see you. She was mad as a cat that night. Boy, did you ever take off running! You shoulda seen yourself."

"So what'd you do?"

He laughed again. I was getting tired of it.

"I watched you run is what I did. Old Red—that's Henderson's old mutt—he ain't never bit nobody."

"Yeah, well, thanks for telling me."

"Andie, she was all heated up over it. Said it was a mean thing to do. You still mad?"

"Nah." I was, but not too mad.

"Well, we was just kids, y'know. So what do you say? Let's drop in on Andie. I was going up there anyways."

By that time we were a good mile past Boggs's End, and I wasn't interested in heading back down that road just then with the Gleason clan in pursuit, so I said okay.

Andie lived about three miles up the road in a sprawling, dilapidated farmhouse, pigs and chickens running loose everywhere. A couple of the pigs came running up to the car. I hesitated, not liking the look of the one snuffling outside my door.

"She ain't gonna hurt ya," Scud said, climbing out his side. "Just lookin' for food."

I still didn't like it. I remembered the peanut butter sandwich in my pocket, unwrapped it, and sailed it out across the farmyard. The pig took off after it. I got out of the car and followed Scud toward the house. Now that we were out of the car, I noticed he'd gotten taller since I'd last seen him. He must've been close to six and a half feet.

Andie was sitting on the porch shucking sweet corn.

"Hey, Andie," Scud said.

Her yellow cotton dress had little blue polka dots all over it. She stood up, leaned against one of the porch pillars, and crossed her arms. Her red hair was tied back, loose and full. Freckles spattered her sun-browned skin. I remembered her as a wiry kid with sharp knuckles. She wasn't so wiry anymore. Her dress was maybe a size too small, her body pushing against it in all the right ways. I almost forgot to breathe. She smiled, and her white teeth cut right to my heart.

"Who you got there, Scudderoo?" I could feel her voice in my chest, deep and clear.

"This here's your friend Jack. You remember Jack, doncha? He runs like a deer." Scud let loose again with that irritating laugh.

Andie peered more closely at me, shading her green eyes with one hand, then stretched her lips into an impish grin. "Is that Jack?"

"That's me."

Scud said, "Where's your old man?"

Andie tilted her head. "Out cuttin' hay." She looked at me again. Every time she did that I got this buzz running up through my body. "You hungry? I got a pot of soup goin' inside."

We were hungry. Andie served us up huge bowls of chicken soup with thick slices of chewy, tasty bread that she'd baked herself. I couldn't keep my eyes off her. Scud told her that I was a fugitive from the Gleasons.

"They looked like they was likely to lynch him," he said.

"What did you do?" Andie wanted to know.

My instincts told me not to tell them where I was from, but I really wanted to impress Andie, so I reached into my pocket and fished out another quarter.

"Looks sort of odd," Andie said. "Looks like it ain't real silver."

Scud examined the coin. "Is it a phony?" He held the quarter closer to his face. "Nineteen ninety-three? Not a very good counterfeit, they can't even get the date right."

"It's no counterfeit," I said. "I'm from the future."

He gave me a look, then burst into laughter.

Andie started laughing, too. "You had him going for a second there, Jackie," she said.

Just then, the door banged open and a tall, gray-haired man wearing soiled overalls stepped into the kitchen. He glared at Scud.

Scud stood up. "Good afternoon, Mr. Murphy."

He snorted, then said to Andie, "Feeding the pigs again, eh, girl?"

I thought he was talking about us, but Andie gave out a squeak and ran out the door. The pigs had gotten into the corn she'd been shucking. Mr. Murphy watched her through the door, a bemused expression on his weather-lined face. After a few seconds, she came back inside, her face red with anger and embarrassment.

Mr. Murphy grinned, showing us his set of enormous white teeth. "I'm s'prised there's any left, girl, what with you feeding the animals with one hand and your friends with t'other."

"Sorry, Daddy." She noticed he was staring at me. "Daddy, this is Jack."

He looked me up and down. "Never seen ya b'fore," he said.

"I'm just passing through."

"Drifter, huh? You lookin' for work?"

"Not just now."

"On account a I got work. I got more work 'n you can shake a stick at. Now Franklin here"—he indicated Scud with a jerk of his head—"he don't believe in work, do ya, son?"

Scud grinned uncomfortably. Andie was setting out another bowl of soup.

"He'd rather be gallivanting 'round in that old jalopy a his, scaring hell out of the animals." Mr. Murphy took a seat at the table. "You boys done eating my food? 'Cause if you are, I don't mind you hit the road. Me'n Andrea here, we got a farm to run."

Scud and I made our way out the door. We'd just got into Scud's Ford when Andie came out, tried to kick one of the pigs, missed, then ran up to the car. She looked quickly back at the house, then threw her arms around Scud's neck, planted a loud kiss on his lips, then ran back into the house.

That kiss echoed like a shattered gong in my chest. As we drove away, Scud said, "Me and her, we're gonna get married once she turns eighteen."

I felt like throwing up.

I made him drop me off at Boggs's End.

"What you want to go there for?" he wanted to know. "Ain't nobody lived there since the Boggses. That was really something, them disappearing like that."

"What do you think happened?"

"I dunno. Some people say they went to California. Me, I figure they maybe got murdered and buried in the woods someplace."

"How come you figure that?"

"What else? They wouldn't a just left their house and all their stuff behind. The bank, they sold off all the furniture, but nobody wanted to buy the house so they just let it go for taxes. Look, why don't you stay with me? My ma won't mind."

"That's okay. I want to stay here."

"Well, don't disappear like the Boggses." He grinned, and for a moment his face seemed familiar.

I opened the car door and stepped out, then turned and took a closer look at him. "How come you get called Scud?"

He seemed surprised at the question. "That's my name, why d'ya think?"

"Cause Mr. Murphy called you Franklin."

"My last name's Scudder, okay? Only thing I ever got from my old man."

I shut the door. "Thanks for the ride."

Franklin Scudder waved and drove off.

And I came back through the door.

## My Father Returns

Mom found a job in Lake City working for a pick-your-own-berries farmer. It was a temporary job and it didn't pay much, but she was happy to get it, and we got lots of free berries. A few weeks later someone knocked on the front door. Mom was literally up to her elbows in raspberry preserves, so I answered it. It was a delivery guy with the biggest bouquet of flowers I'd seen since Skoro's funeral. I looked at the note attached.

*These roses are red*
*But I'm feeling blue*
*I'm off the sauce now*
*And I really miss you.*
*—Ronnie*

I was thinking about hauling the bouquet out to the compost bin when Mom came up behind me wiping her hands on a towel.

"For me?" she said.

It made me sick to hear the hope in her voice.

I didn't say anything, just handed her the roses and went up to my room.

Dad showed up at Boggs's End three days later.

"How's it going, champ?" he said, faking a punch at my shoulder. He'd shaved off his mustache and put on a few pounds.

"Okay, I guess." I didn't look at his eyes. The thing was, I was glad to see him, but at the same time I was mad at myself. I'd tried to forget him, to write him out of my life, but he was my dad and it's pretty amazing what a dad can do and still have you like him.

He said he hadn't had a drink since the day they let him out of jail. Since then, he'd been driving a delivery van and going to AA meetings seven nights a week. He said he hadn't called us before because he was ashamed, and he wanted to be absolutely sure he had his drinking problem licked before he saw either of us again. He said it had been the hardest three months of his life. We were sitting at the kitchen table listening when the strangest thing happened.

He started crying.

Now, I know that men cry sometimes, and there's nothing wrong with it, but to see *my* father cry, it was like the sky had turned from blue to red-and-green polka dot. I'd never before seen him with so much as a teary eye, and here he was snuffling like a lost child.

After that, there wasn't much to say. Of course, Mom said he could stay.

The next morning they were all lovey-dovey, like nothing bad had ever happened between them. I walked into the living room and found them sitting tight together on the sofa, smiling like Romeo and Juliet. It made me feel good, but more than that it made me feel weird. I came right out and said it.

"Hanging out with you guys is like being in the Twilight Zone."

There was a time when if I said something like that my father would've smacked me and my mom would've started crying. But it didn't faze them. Dad laughed, and Mom sort of let her head fall on his shoulder.

I took my baseball bat and went out to the orchard to hit the wormy apples. I liked the sound they made when splattered by a hard-swung aluminum bat.

In the mornings, Mom would go to her job at the berry farm, and Dad and I would go to work on Boggs's End. A house that big, there's always plenty to do. We replaced cracked windows, unstuck stuck doors, scraped and repainted the veranda, fixed the loose banister at the top of the stairs, put new washers in the leaking bathroom faucet. We went to work outside, too, cutting back the young walnut and ash trees that were invading the orchard, and trimming dead wood off the apple trees. Mom wanted us to put up a clothesline so she could dry the laundry outdoors, so we found some rope in one of the sheds and strung it up between two of the apple trees. As he pulled the rope tight, my dad looked critically at the misshapen fruit weighing down the branches.

"Too late to do anything about them this year, champ. If we haven't sold the place by spring, we'll start spraying them. That's when you have to stop the worms. Next year maybe we can make cider, if we don't sell this place first."

"Does Mom want to sell the house now?" I wasn't sure which way I wanted him to answer.

Dad stood with the pruning saw in his hand, staring up into the twisted branches. "I don't know, Jack. What do you think? It's going to be a long winter. You want to spend it here?"

"Mom likes it."

"Are you sure? Maybe what she liked was just being away from me while I was drinking. She liked it in Skokie as long as I was on the wagon."

These conversations made me uncomfortable.

"I don't care," I said. That usually stopped a conversation

dead. It worked like a charm. Dad pressed his lips together and went after another limb with his saw.

We finished the orchard, then cut back the hydrangeas that were taking over the south side of the house. I hacked at the fibrous stems with hedge clippers and tried not to look too hard at the door-shaped patch of mismatched siding.

# The Invisible Man

One afternoon I was sitting in the study flipping through some of Skoro's old copies of *National Geographic* when I looked out the window and saw my mother in the orchard talking to somebody. But there was no one there. She stood holding her basket of wet laundry, shirts and towels hanging from our improvised clothesline, talking to some invisible person, smiling too hard the way she would when meeting someone new. It gave me a hard-to-describe feeling, something like having your body climbed by a thousand ice-cold centipedes. The one-sided conversation didn't last long—she slowly rotated her head as if she was watching someone walk away, then let go of the laundry basket with one hand and waved. The basket fell. Wet laundry spilled onto the grass.

That night at dinner, as she was shaking Parmesan cheese over her spaghetti, my mom mentioned that we'd had a visitor.

"That older gentleman we saw at the funeral. You remember him, Ron. He had an eye patch?"

That brought the centipedes back.

"What did he want?" Dad asked.

"He was hunting mushrooms. He said his name was Mr. Was."

"I don't like it. He's got no business coming on our property."

"He seemed harmless enough, Ron. I told him he was welcome to hunt mushrooms on our land."

Dad frowned and spun a wad of spaghetti onto his fork. "I don't like it," he mumbled, his mouth full of noodles. "The guy gives me the creeps."

The whole situation was giving *me* the creeps.

I rode my bike down the hill to Ole's one afternoon, just looking for something to do. I figured I'd play some pinball, maybe rent a video. The Gleason twins were sitting on their usual stools, nursing their beers, looking as dumb and old and ugly as ever. They still hadn't figured out how come I looked so familiar, and I wasn't about to remind them. Ole slouched behind the counter, a smoldering cigarette between his nicotine-yellowed fingers.

"Well if it ain't the master of Boggs's End," he said.

"That's right," I said. It didn't pay to argue with Ole, I'd learned. He was a jerk, and pretty much everybody in town knew it, but since he owned the only retail operation within ten miles, people put up with him.

"I hear your old man's doing a lot a work up there."

"We're all working on it."

"He stopped by this morning, talking about how your granddaddy let everything go to hell. Sounds like he left you with a real rat hole."

I didn't like that, him calling our place a rat hole, but I knew he was just trying to get under my skin, so I walked over to the video rack and tried to find a movie I hadn't already seen twice. It was hard to concentrate, though, because something else was bothering me worse than Ole's insults. Dad had left that morning to go into Rochester to rent some scaffolding so we could start painting up under the eaves.

Why had he driven down the hill to Ole's?

I didn't have to wonder long.

Ole said, "You tell your daddy, next time you see him, you tell him I'll be stocking his brand from here on out. Okay?"

"What brand is that?"

"That fancy lemon vodka he likes, son. Appears my house brand ain't good enough for you city folk."

I got on my bike and started pedaling. I'd just got up to speed when suddenly I ran into something and went flying through the air and landed flat on my back. For what seemed like a long time I lay staring up at the cloudless blue, feeling the road pressing up against my body, trying to get some air into my flattened lungs. When I was finally able to sit up, I looked to see what I'd hit. There was only my bicycle, handlebars twisted to one side, chain broken.

But I knew I'd run into something. Or somebody. Somebody invisible.

I walked my broken bike all the way up the bluff to Boggs's End, arriving long after the sun had set. Dad's car was still gone. Mom sat alone at the kitchen table, three places set, all the food still in its serving dishes. She hadn't touched a thing.

I wasn't hungry, but I sat down and helped myself to cold mashed potatoes, cold pork chops, warm milk. Once I started eating, Mom took one of the pork chops, cut off a small piece, chewed it slowly. She was staring at Dad's empty plate.

I can't explain to you how she knew. There was a time when she might have thought he'd had a flat tire, or that he'd gotten lost, or broken down, or killed in an accident. Not anymore. I didn't even have to tell her about what Ole had said. She knew.

All of a sudden Mom picked up Dad's plate and sailed it through the kitchen door like a Frisbee, all the way into the living room where it hit the chandelier with the sound of a thousand breaking glasses. The plate and a good part of the chandelier crashed to the floor. Glass shards were everywhere.

I said, "Mom?"

"No more," she said, her face white and hard. "I'm not going through it again." She got up and put the chain on the front door, then did the same to the back.

"Maybe he'll just go back to Skokie," I said.

She shook her head. "He'll be back. But he won't get in."

## The Car in the Foyer

She was half right.

I lay awake in bed that night until well past midnight, waiting. Sometime around two I fell asleep. At about four o'clock in the morning I woke up to the sound of the door banging against its chain, hard and repeatedly.

I could hear his hoarse shouts, then my mother's footsteps. I tugged on a pair of jeans, shoved my feet into my Nikes, opened my bedroom door. Mom stood halfway down the stairs, looking at the front door.

"Don't talk to him, Mom," I said. "Let him yell." She didn't answer, just stood there holding her bathrobe closed with one hand, gripping the banister with the other, staring down the staircase.

I knew if she listened to him too long she wouldn't be able to resist. She would go down and yell back at him through the crack in the door. That was part of the problem. She couldn't help but listen to him, to his foul accusations and crude insults. When he called her names she couldn't just walk away, couldn't leave it alone, even when it meant she would get hurt. He knew how to punch her buttons, and she responded like a trained animal.

She started down the stairs. I ran after her and grabbed her arm.

"Get off me!" she snapped, as if I was my father, then shook me off with a violent shudder. I watched her descend the stairs, feeling helpless and angry at both of them.

The hell with them, I thought. Let them fight. They could kill each other, for all I cared. I went back to my room, sat on my bed, and waited for the explosion.

I didn't have to wait long.

First, there was the predictable exchange of hoarse profanities. Most of it was coming from my father, but Mom was getting in her licks, too. Having a chained door between them seemed to inspire her. Then there was a minute or so when I heard only my mother's voice, then about thirty seconds of silence. Then the roar of an engine, screeching tires, and a tremendous crash—the sound of splintering wood and breaking glass.

My mother screamed.

I heard a car door slam.

I couldn't just sit there in my room. I don't remember grabbing my baseball bat, but I must've because when I got downstairs it was in my hands.

The front end of Dad's Jeep was in the foyer. The double front doors we had just refinished had been blasted open, one of them torn off its hinges.

I could hear them in the kitchen, my father's voice hoarse with rage, my mother saying, "Go away, leave us alone! Go away, leave us alone!"

I came around the corner.

She had a knife, holding it in both hands, waving it back and forth.

My father had a chair in his hands, holding it out like a lion tamer. He jabbed at her with the legs, then swung it hard, knocking the knife away. He dropped the chair and fell on her with his fists, hitting her on the face and shoulders, driving her down onto the floor.

I let out a yell and charged him with the baseball bat held high, swinging it down as hard as I could. He heard me, twisted his body, dove to the side. The bat caught him on the hip, but he somehow got his hands on it and wrenched it from my grasp. I backed away. My mother was curled up on the floor, her arms locked over her head.

He limped toward me, his face blotchy red with fury.

"You little blindsiding coward. You sneaking little bastard. C'mere, you little piece a crap. Let's see how you like it."

I thought I was going to die.

I backed away from him, out of the kitchen, down the hall. He kept coming, his fingers white on the bat handle. I turned and ran up the stairs. He climbed after me. I figured my only chance would be to head for the third floor, to go back through the short door. I was on my way up when I heard my mother's voice.

"You leave him alone!"

"Shut up and stay out of this!" he shouted in a hoarse voice.

"I won't let you hurt him, Ron."

"Put that down!"

Sounds of a scuffle, a grunt, and then a sound I'll never forget as long as I live, a sound both soft and sharp, like the sound of a dropped melon, followed by the thud of a body hitting the floor, then the metallic clatter of an aluminum baseball bat, then silence.

I heard only the blood whooshing through the arteries in my head. Slowly, quietly, I descended the stairs and looked out into the hallway.

She was staring up at me, her head twisted to the side, eyes unblinking, the side of her head—

The side of her head—

The side of her head in a pool of growing red, touching the sole of his shoe. The bat on the floor, wet red. My eyes went from her eyes to the blood to the bat to his shoe to his spattered pant leg up his body to his slack-jawed face, drained of all color, eyes protruding.

He said, "She made me do it."

I fell forward onto my knees and threw up. My mother. My bat. I wanted him to pick it up and kill me, too. I didn't want to live. I pressed my forehead to the wooden floor.

Kill me, too, I thought.

I felt him walk away. I heard his feet on the stairs.

I stayed where I was, my eyes squeezed shut, trying to stop time, to reverse it, to hold back the pain and the horror that threatened to drown me. I felt as if I were hanging over an abyss, as if to relax one single muscle would plunge me into the deep. Thoughts flapped about in the dark inside my head like a colony of frightened bats unable to land.

Did time pass? It must have, because when I finally uncurled and opened my eyes the window at the end of the hall was yellow-gray with early sunlight. I could hear the birds singing their morning songs . . . and I could hear my father's voice.

I stood up without looking at what lay beside me and walked to the window.

My father stood in the orchard, talking to the invisible man. He pointed at himself, he pointed at the house, his mouth moved. He started to take down the clothesline. I could see his face clearly. I could see the shine of tears beneath his eyes. He looked drawn, as if the crying had drained his body fluids, as if only his dried husk remained.

I tried to hate him, but I had nothing left inside. There was no anger, no pain, no sensation whatsoever. I didn't even wonder why he was untying the clothesline.

All I cared about was what I had to do next.

# I Go Back Again

I stepped through the metal door into night, starless and black and bitter cold, only the faintest trace of light from town rising over the bluff. A steady wind sucked the heat out of me. I shuffled around the house through a dusting of brittle snow, pulled a board off the window leading into the kitchen, and climbed through. The inside of the house wasn't any warmer, but at least there was no wind.

I'd had the sense to throw on my down parka and a stocking cap, but I hadn't thought to bring a flashlight. I found a box of matches in one of the cupboards. I walked through the empty rooms, lighting one match after another, the flickering flames throwing weird shadows against the peeling wallpaper.

I spent most of the night in front of the fireplace, burning scraps of paper, curtains, and hunks of an old broken chair, and whatever else I could find. I fell asleep once, but soon awakened with the image of my mother's battered head floating in front of my eyes. A couple times I almost went back through the door, but the memory of what I'd find there kept me in place.

It was a long, cold, miserable night. Morning arrived icy and gray. As soon as it was light enough to see, I set off up the road toward Andie's. It was the only place I knew to go.

I almost froze to death. Last time I'd been there Scud had been driving. On foot it wasn't so close. My ears, toes, and fingers had all gone numb by the time I banged on their door.

Nobody answered. I pushed the door open. Warm, moist air. I shouted, "Anybody home?"

No answer. I stepped inside, unzipped my parka with clumsy, half-frozen fingers, and let the heat penetrate.

When Andie's father got home half an hour later, I was sitting at his kitchen table eating a loaf of his daughter's homebaked bread.

He did not seem pleased to see me.

Old man Murphy turned out to be an okay guy, once he got over the shock of finding me in his kitchen. I had to tell him something, and he wouldn't have believed the whole truth, so I made up the story as I went along, sprinkling the lies with bits of fact. I told him I'd hitchhiked up from Chicago looking for a job. I told him my mother was dead. Saying it out loud felt like coughing up a softball—my throat clamped down and I started to cry. The old man just sat there looking at me all stony faced, trying to figure out what to do with me.

I knew he wasn't going to send me back out in the cold. It would have been like sentencing me to death. After I managed to get hold of myself, he asked me what kind of work I was looking for.

"Any kind," I said. "Why?"

"On account of I could use an extra hand around here." He held up his right arm and, for the first time, I noticed his wrist was swollen up to about twice its normal size.

"Just tell me what to do," I said.

What I remember most about those first days on the Murphy farm is the numbness in my brain. My mind had just turned itself off, and I went through the motions without much using the thinking part of my brain. I didn't want to think, I didn't want to remember. I wanted to pretend it had all been a dream. Everything. I imagined that my entire body was shot full of Novocain. I wore the numbness like a shield. Nothing could get in, and I would let nothing out.

Each morning I would wake up to a banging on the cellar door. I would sit up in my cot wrapped in the prickly, ugly green wool army blankets, cold cellar air swirling around me. I would get dressed in the long johns, flannel shirt, and denim overalls that the old man had given to me. I would report to the kitchen table, where Andie would have laid out a big farm breakfast of pancakes, eggs, sausages, bacon, bread, biscuits, coffee cake, and apple cider. The old man would already have it half eaten. I would sit down and start eating, and I would keep eating until he growled that it was time to get to work.

I went through the motions, letting the old man order me around, content to be told what to do. He worked me like a slave, always yelling and watching and telling me how everything I did was wrong. Since I was numb anyways, it didn't much matter to me. I just did what he told me and, after the first week, the old man slacked off and started treating me like I was a human being. But I still had to work my butt off.

A lot of the work seemed to involve shoveling large quantities of manure. Fifty percent of farming is feeding the animals. The other half is cleaning up after them, shoveling their crap. In fact, that was what the old man had been doing when he'd slipped and fallen and sprained his wrist.

It was hard work, but right then hard work was what I needed. I wanted to stay busy, to exhaust my body, to get so tired that when I finally fell into my cot at the end of the day I'd be too tired to think, too tired to remember.

I wanted time to pass.

About fifty-five years.

Because that was how long I'd have to wait to undo my mother's death.

What is most interesting to me now, looking back on that time in my life, is how quickly the memory of my mother's murder faded from my thoughts. It was not that I forgot it—how could I ever forget such a thing?—it was more that the memory lost its intensity. It was still there in my mind, but without the harsh edges, without the horror, without the power to twist my mind into an agonized knot. As each hour on the Murphy farm passed, the memory of that horrible day seemed to recede into my past by days or weeks.

I now know that this softening of memory is common to those who pass through time. It does not seem to matter whether they travel through time a day at a time, or pass through a fifty-five-year door. The effect remains the same. The memories never completely disappear, but they become as distant as a remembered dream, and as changeable.

# My Date with Scud and Andie

My mind is full of boxes. Places I can store things that I do not want to look at too closely or too often.

My mother's death was in one box, the fact that my father had killed her was in another. And ever since I'd found out that Andie was Scud's girlfriend, I'd tried to put her in a box, too, but she wouldn't stay there. We were living in the same house. I saw her every day.

And every time I looked at her face, my insides would melt all over again.

Fortunately, I didn't see much of her during the day. The old man kept me busy, and she would be at school or running errands in town or busy in the kitchen cooking. But mealtimes were bad. We would sit across from each other at the kitchen table. I tried to keep from staring at her, but sometimes I just couldn't help it. She had a glow on her that pulled at my eyes the way a lightbulb grabs hold of a bug. To make things even worse, the old man would be there watching us both, his head swiveling back and forth. Sometimes Andie would catch me staring right at her, which made me blush, which made her laugh, which made the old man start talking in an overloud voice about whatever was on his mind, be it cow manure, the price of plug tobacco, or the war in Europe.

The first time I heard him mention the war in Europe, I'd said, "You mean World War Two?"

He shook his head. “Won’t be no World War Two,” he said. “We’re stayin’ out of this one like we shoulda stayed out of the big one.”

“But what about Pearl Harbor?” I asked.

He gave me the blankest look you can imagine. “Pearl what?” he said.

I had to literally bite my tongue. I hadn’t been much of a history student, but I remembered that World War II had started up when the Japanese attacked Pearl Harbor. For a moment I wanted to tell him, to warn him of what was to come, but I knew it would be a mistake. I was living in this time now, not a time when World War II was ancient history. Even if he believed me, which he wouldn’t, what good would it do for him to know that the Japanese were going to attack Pearl Harbor? What could he do? Call the president?

This wasn’t my world, anyway. I hadn’t even been born yet. I was just a visitor. Besides, I couldn’t remember the date the attack was supposed to happen. I couldn’t even remember the year.

“This is real good chicken, Andie,” I said, trying to change the subject.

“Why, thank you, Jack.”

“Andie always makes good chicken,” her father growled, tearing into a thigh with his long white teeth, giving me a look like I shouldn’t say nice things to his daughter.

After supper Andie would do her homework, or sometimes she would sew buttons or patches on clothing. I would sit and read. I was making my way through a stack of old *Saturday Evening Posts*, trying to get a feel for life in 1941. The old man would turn on the radio to listen to Amos and Andy or Burns and Allen or Jack Benny. When he heard something he thought was funny he’d slap his thigh and laugh so sharp and loud it could stop your heart if you weren’t expecting it.

The old man was fascinated by my down-filled ripstop nylon parka. He'd sit in his chair rolling the bright blue fabric between his fingers saying, "Never seen nothing like it. You say you got this in Chicago?"

"That's right," I said.

"Wonder if they have such a thing up in Minneapolis."

"I don't know," I said. I had no idea what they had in Minneapolis in 1941.

"Looks expensive," he said.

"I don't know." I really wanted to change the subject, but now that he'd got me thinking about the future I decided to ask a question that had been on my mind. "Say," I said, "is there a family around here named Skoro?"

"Skoro?" the old man blinked and sat back in his chair. "Skoro? Sounds sort of familiar, but I don't believe so." He looked over at Andie. "You know any Skoros hereabouts, girl?"

Andie shook her head. "Never heard of no Skoro."

The old man squinted at me, his head against the back of his rocker. "Why you askin'?"

I shrugged. "I heard there was some Skoros living up here."

"Relatives a yours?"

"Just a name I heard my mom mention once. Before she died."

He pressed his lips together and moved his chin slowly up and down, his eyes fixed on mine. "That's a hard thing, to lose your mama."

I heard Andie get up and walk into the kitchen.

"But I don't know no Skoro. Not that I know every blessed person in the county."

"No big deal," I said, both relieved and confused. I was sure that Mom had said that Grandpa Skoro had grown up in Memory. Maybe he'd moved here later on.

"But I hear of any, I'll tell you so."

Or maybe he had never lived here. Maybe I had traveled to someone else's past.

One thing we didn't talk about much was Scud. Every once in a while his name would come up, but the old man made it pretty clear he did not like Franklin Scudder, so Andie didn't talk about him much.

I'd been on the farm three days the first time Scud stopped by. I remember he walked into the barn where, as usual, I was shoveling manure.

"Hey," he said. "Is that Jack the apple thief? Or is it Jack the counterfeiter?" He wore a long, mouse-colored wool coat over a clean chambray shirt and dark brown pants. Except for the huge zit on his chin, he looked like a movie star. His checkered porkpie hat was cocked one way, his wide smile the other. It was hard to not like a guy who could smile like that.

I stopped shoveling and stuck the pitchfork in the wheelbarrow full of dung, conscious of my grimy overalls with the rolled-up cuffs and one broken suspender. I wiped my forehead with my sleeve.

"It's Jack the shit shoveler," I said. "How you doing?"

"I'm doing great." He looked around the barn like he'd never seen one before. "First time I ever seen you you wasn't outside getting chased."

I shrugged.

"So where you been?"

"Just wandering," I said.

Scud hiked himself up onto the railing of a stall. The cow inside snorted and shuffled. "Andie tells me the old man's really got you bustin' your butt here. Looks like she told me right."

"I'm helping him out, just till his hand gets better."

"Long as he's got you to do his work for him, he ain't gonna get better."

"Maybe." There was some tension between us. On my side, I knew where it was coming from. I'd been thinking about Andie pretty much twenty-four hours a day, and I'd been trying not to think about Scud.

He dug in a pocket of his clean blue cotton shirt and pulled out a pack of Lucky Strikes. "You want one?"

"No thanks. Those things can give you lung cancer."

Scud gave me a puzzled look. "What's that?"

"Lung cancer. You get it and you die."

He lit up with a wooden match, blew a stream of blue smoke at me. "You're nuts, you know that?"

"So I'm nuts. That cigarette is still gonna kill you."

"I suppose you're gonna tell me that in the future nobody smokes."

My guard went up. "What do you mean?"

"You said you were from the future."

"I was kidding."

Scud took a drag off his Lucky. "I knew that," he said.

Scud showed up a couple times a week, usually around mealtimes, usually dressed up like he had someplace important to be. He was there to see Andie, of course, but he liked to take a few minutes to watch me work. I think he was worried about me and Andie being around each other so much.

One day, while Scud was watching me replace a broken board on the side of the barn, he came right out with it. "So what do you think about Andie?" he asked.

"She's okay." I was working with a handful of rusty, bent nails. Old man Murphy said new nails were too expensive, so I was trying to straighten out the old nails using a hammer and a brick.

"Me and her, we're going to get married as soon as she's done with school."

"You mentioned." I was holding a nail with one hand against the brick. You had to get the nail in just the right position, then give it a good smack on the side. With a little luck, it would straighten out just good enough so it would pound into a board.

"Just wanted to make sure you knew. You know?"

I'd got the nail nearly straight, took one more hard swing at it, and smashed the tip of my finger. I dropped the hammer, jumped up, and howled.

Scud started laughing. That did it. I tackled him, and we both tumbled into the muddy track that led from the barn out into the pasture where the cattle grazed. We rolled over each other a couple times, then I got on top and pinned him to the ground. His wool coat and most of the rest of him was covered with mud.

"You think it's funny?" My finger was throbbing.

"Jeez, Jack, would'ja take it easy?"

"It's not funny."

"Okay, okay, it's not funny. Get off me, would'ja?" He had a big glob of muck stuck to his forehead. All of a sudden I saw what we must've looked liked, two guys rolling around in the muck and cow pie. I tried to stand up, slipped in the mud, and went down again, landing hard on my butt. Scud started laughing, and the glob of mud on his forehead rolled down his face onto his chest. That set us both off. When the old man came around the corner of the barn, we were both laughing so hard I was afraid I was going to pee in my pants. Not that it would have made any difference at that point. Old man Murphy just shook his head, turned, and walked away.

For some reason, both Scud and I thought that was about the funniest thing we'd ever seen.

That was the thing about Scud. He could be a real jerk, but he knew how to have a good time.

A few days after the mud incident, I was getting ready to clean out some of the stalls when Scud showed up in a corn-colored trench coat and a wide-brimmed felt hat with a feather stuck in the band. I invited him to help me out.

"No thanks," he said. "I don't do manual labor."

I made a move like I was going to tackle him. He backed away, saying, "New coat! New coat!"

We had a laugh over that.

Scud said, "Me and Andie, we're driving into Red Wing tonight to see an Abbott and Costello movie."

"That's nice."

"You got thirty cents, you can come along."

I had about twenty dollars in 1990s money, but here in 1941 I couldn't spend a dime of it without getting arrested. I figured I could get some money from old man Murphy, since he owed me for the time I'd worked, but the idea of being a third wheel on Scud and Andie's date didn't appeal to me. I was about to tell him no thanks when I all of a sudden had this image of the two of them sitting in the back row of the theater, making out like crazy. If I was there, they'd have to behave themselves.

"Sure," I said. "That sounds okay."

"Show's at seven. I'll pick you up around six." He gave my grimy overalls a critical look. "You got something besides that you can wear?"

"Don't worry about it," I said. "I'll get out my tuxedo."

Later I found out the only reason he'd invited me was that the old man wouldn't let Andie go to the movies with just Scud. I was supposed to be their chaperone. I think if her father had thought he could get away with it, he'd have forbidden Andie to see Scud at all. But the old man was smart enough to know that if he did that, Andie would be sneaking out every chance she got.

Scud showed up a few minutes after six. Andie and I were all ready to go, but Mr. Murphy was still finishing his dessert. Scud pulled his Ford right up to the front porch and leaned on his horn. Andie got up and started for the door.

Mr. Murphy looked up from his pie and said, "Hold it right there, girl. You wait for him to come knocking, as is proper."

Andie rolled her eyes at me, but came back and sat at the table.

It took Scud a good two minutes to figure it out, but finally we heard his footsteps on the porch and his knock on the door.

Mr. Murphy pointed his fork at me, then at the door. I went to answer it.

Scud was decked out in his new coat, a bright red scarf, and his felt hat. He looked like the Shadow, only with blue eyes and that pimple on his chin.

Andie wore a plain green dress. An ugly dress, I thought, but somehow it made her more beautiful than ever, her red hair shiny and full, her green eyes dancing with energy.

I had on a clean pair of overalls, my Nikes, and my nylon parka. Scud gave me a critical once-over. "Where'd you get those shoes?"

"Chicago," I said. It had been enough of an explanation for old man Murphy.

"They look like clown shoes," he said.

"They walk just fine."

"Let's go!" Andie said. "We don't want to be late."

"Movie don't start till seven," said Mr. Murphy.

"We want to get the good seats," Scud said. He picked

Andie's often-mended coat from the hanger behind the door and held it open for her.

Mr. Murphy glared at him, then said to Andie, "You be home by eleven, girl." He turned to me. "You make sure," he said.

We all promised to be good, then it was out the door and into Scud's Ford, the three of us crowded into the front seat with Andie in the middle. I liked the feel of that, Andie's hip pressed against mine. But she was leaning more toward Scud. I just set my jaw and tried not to think about it.

On the way to Red Wing we stopped at a roadhouse where Scud tried to buy some beer. While Scud was in the roadhouse making a fool of himself, Andie and I got a chance to talk.

"I thought we were just going to a movie," I said.

Andie grinned at me. Her coat was old and worn, but the way that collar framed her face, especially sitting outside the beer joint with the red and white lights from the entryway lighting up her features, it was a beautiful thing to see. Her eyes, green by daylight, now looked as dark and deep and thick as pools of molasses.

"He's just showin' off," she said. "Trying to impress you."

"How do you know he's not trying to impress *you?*"

"Scud knows he's not gonna impress me. Anyways, he doesn't have to. We known each other a long time." I thought I detected a touch of regret in her voice, but it might have been my imagination.

She went on, "They won't sell him any beer in there anyways. I could've told him that, on account of my cousin Teddy works the bar and he knows Scud's not of age. But it doesn't pay to argue with Scud. You get to know him better, you'll find that out." She wrinkled her nose. "But one thing for sure, he isn't boring."

Andie was right on all counts. Scud wasn't in the roadhouse two minutes before they kicked him out. He opened the door and got behind the wheel, saying, "Bunch of country jerks." I didn't say anything to Scud, but I was glad he hadn't gotten the beer. I didn't want to be drinking beer, not after seeing what it did to my father, and I didn't want to be riding around in a car being driven by a drunken Scud. I got the impression that Andie wasn't too disappointed, either.

So we got to the Metro theater in Red Wing in plenty of time to buy a couple boxes of popcorn for a nickel each and grab the "good seats" which, according to Andie, were the ones in the front row. She said she liked to fill her eyes up with the movie and nothing else. The lights went down a few seconds after we took our seats, Andie sitting between me and Scud, and the newsreel started up.

Movie theaters don't have newsreels anymore, not since television got started. But back then, just about any movie you went to would start out with a newsreel, a five-minute movie about something that was happening in the world. This one was about the war in Europe. It showed German tanks rolling across Eastern Europe, columns of war prisoners, fleets of destroyers in the North Sea, soldiers firing mortars, all with this hokey-sounding drum music in the background and an announcer with a super-deep voice going on about "Hitler's war machine" and "courageous British defenders." One clip showed the president, Franklin Roosevelt, saying that the United States would not be drawn into needless conflict. Knowing as I did that the United States would soon be in the thick of it, I could feel the hair standing up on the back of my neck.

Right about then, I got hit with the first piece of popcorn.

I didn't know what it was, I just felt something bounce off my head.

The newsreel ended and a cartoon came on. I noticed Andie give a little jerk, then brush at her hair. I turned around to look behind us. Two rows back, three guys about our age sat grinning at us. I smiled back at them uncertainly, thinking that they might be friends of Scud or Andie, then I recognized two of them: Harry and Hermie, the twins from Gleason's Market. The other kid, older and bigger than the twins, flicked another kernel at me but missed. Andie put her hand on my wrist. "Ignore them, Jack," she whispered.

Scud leaned over. "What's going on?" he asked.

"Nothing," Andie said. "Watch the movie."

A piece of popcorn bounced off her head and fell onto her lap. Scud looked back at the popcorn throwers and started to get up. Andie grabbed his arm and pulled him back down. "Don't start anything, Scud. Please! The movie's starting. Hush up and watch it!"

So we watched the movie. Every few minutes a popcorn kernel would fall among us. Each time that happened, Andie would give my hand a squeeze. It wasn't a bad trade-off, but I sure wasn't able to concentrate on the movie, which was pretty silly, anyway. I had never seen an Abbott and Costello movie before, and I wasn't sure I ever wanted to see another one. After a while, the popcorn bombardment stopped, either because they got tired of throwing the kernels, or because they ran out of popcorn. A little later, Scud whispered something to Andie, got up, and left the theater.

"Where's he going?" I whispered.

"He says he thinks he left the headlights on," Andie whispered back, her lips only inches from my ear. She smelled of popcorn and Ivory soap.

I let my eyes watch the movie, but my mind was completely focused on my left arm where Andie's hand was resting.

I didn't even notice when Scud returned to his seat, but later when I looked over he was there, staring up at the movie screen, a strange sort of smile pasted across his face.

I had the feeling he'd done something that was going to get us in trouble.

I was right.

# CHERRY BOMBS

After the movie ended, Andie made us sit in our seats until the popcorn throwers had left the theater. Scud just smiled and sat back in his seat.

"Who was the big guy?" I asked.

"That was Henry, the older brother. I don't get along with them Gleasons so good."

"They think Scud is stealing trade from them," Andie said.

"You mean it was you they were throwing at?" I'd been thinking that all the popcorn throwing had something to do with me trying to buy that comic book with a 1993 quarter.

Scud explained, "They don't like me 'cause I buy stuff and sell it to folks. Like I just drove up to Minneapolis and bought three cases of canned cranberries and four cases of canned pumpkin. On account of Thanksgiving coming up, you know? I got the berries for a nickel a can, and the pie pumpkin for four and a half cents. I can sell those cans door to door in Memory for a dime a can, make myself eight bucks, just like that! People buy from old lady Gleason, it cost 'em fourteen cents. You know? Those Gleasons, they just don't like free trade." He laughed. "They'll be up to their ears in cranberries and pie pumpkin all the way till next fall." It wasn't hard to see why the Gleasons didn't like him much.

Andie said, "Let's go. They're gone."

We filed out of the theater and walked down the block toward the car.

"So is that how you make your money?" I asked.

"That and other stuff."

"Scud's a hustler," Andie said.

"I'm actually a businessman. I do deliveries, all kinds of stuff."

He opened the car door. From up the street came the sound of a revving engine. A beat-up pickup truck pulled away from the curb and raced toward us. As it passed, an arm flew out the window and hurled a beer bottle at us. Scud ducked, the bottle missed his head by inches, bounced off the roof of the Ford, and shattered on the sidewalk. The pickup continued down the street.

"They seem pretty serious," I said after a moment.

Scud had his arms around Andie, holding her tight. I thought she looked uncomfortable. Scud's face was hard and angry. "We'll see who's serious," he said, climbing into the car. Andie and I got in, and we took off.

"You're not going after them, are you?" Andie said.

Scud shifted gears, leaning forward over the wheel.

"Scud?"

"I just want to follow them. I want to see something."

"What's to see?" Andie said. "Let's just go home, Scud. Please?"

"We are going home. This is the way we go to go home."

"Well, don't drive so fast."

"I'm not driving that fast. Besides, I want to show you something."

"Whatever it is, I don't want to see it."

"You'll like it."

"No I won't. Slow down."

I listened to them argue as the speed of the car increased. The speedometer needle stopped at sixty, but we kept picking up speed, racing down the twisted, narrow highway toward

Memory. I didn't know what Scud had in mind, and I knew that Andie was probably right to be cautious, but at the same time I was excited.

The taillights of the pickup appeared in front of us. We got to about a hundred feet behind them, then Scud let up on the gas, matching their speed.

I felt Andie relax as we slowed.

"Now what?" I asked.

"Just watch," Scud said. "Let's see what happens when their muffler gets good and hot."

We stayed close behind the pickup, Scud leaning forward with his chin on the wheel, peering intently through the windshield.

"What did you do, Scudder?" Andie asked. "Did you do something to their truck?"

Scud said, "Who, me?"

Just then the underside of the pickup was lit up by three brilliant yellow flashes followed a split second later by a loud Ba-Ba-BOOM! The back of the pickup seemed to jump off the ground, leaving behind a twisted tailpipe and muffler, and the truck slewed toward the ditch. Andie screamed. Scud wrenched the wheel to the left, narrowly missing the tailpipe, then spun the wheel the other way, just barely staying on the roadway. He pulled over to the shoulder and stopped.

The pickup had rolled down into the ditch and up the other side, then come to a halt in a grove of sumac trees. Scud jockeyed the car around so his headlights shone on the truck.

Henry, Harry, and Hermie staggered out, pale and shaken, but apparently uninjured.

Scud stuck his head out the window. "You fellas okay?"

One of them, I think it was Henry, nodded, too stunned to care that it was Scud asking.

"You see what happened?" he whined. "What happened? We coulda got killed!"

One of the other Gleasons was inspecting the tires, a bewildered expression on his face. "Tires look fine," he said. "Thought we blew every last one of 'em, but they're fine."

Scud said, "That musta been one heck of a backfire. Your muffler and pipe are on the road back there."

"Felt like a bomb went off under the truck," Henry said.

"No kidding?" Scud was grinning so hard I thought he'd tear a cheek. "Maybe somebody shoved a few cherry bombs up your tailpipe."

It took the Gleasons about five seconds to digest that, then their faces lit up and suddenly all three Gleasons were charging at us. Scud, laughing hysterically, revved up the engine. When they were about ten feet away he popped the clutch and the Ford jumped forward—

—and the engine died.

An instant later they'd wrenched open Scud's door and dragged him out. I saw Scud land a fist on one Gleason nose, then he disappeared under their heaving bodies. I tumbled out my door, ran around the car, and dove right in, my fists sinking deep into rolls of Gleason fat. I heard a couple of satisfying squeals before the first blow caught me in the side of my head. For a second I actually saw stars, then the stars turned into Henry Gleason's beady black eyes. I ducked just in time to avoid a second blow. Scud had regained his feet by that time and, elbows and fists whirling, was fighting off both twins at once. Henry, the older brother, had locked his sights on me. He grabbed my arm and swung me hard against the Ford. I bounced off the car door, fell to the ground, and scrambled away on my hands and knees, trying to get enough distance between us so that I could get my feet under me. I looked back in time to see the car door fly open, hitting Henry hard on the hip and knocking him into one of the twins. Then Andie came boiling out of the car and jumped right on top of him, hammering his face with her sharp fists. Henry wrapped his arms over his head and curled up in a ball. I looked back at Scud. The twins had him down on the ground, one of them sitting on his head, the other kicking him hard in the gut. I rammed my shoulder into the kicker's side, and we went tumbling out onto the roadway. I landed a couple, I don't know where, and took an elbow in my right eye. We somehow got to our feet, and started trading punches. He was slow, but it didn't bother him to get hit.

I heard Andie scream.

Apparently, Henry had tired of being beaten up by a girl. He had his big arms wrapped around Andie's waist and was holding her up off the ground. Andie was hollering and kicking and flailing her arms—it looked to me like Henry was still taking the worst of it. I forgot about the twin and went running at him. He saw me coming and let go of Andie. That turned out to be a mistake, because as soon as he let go, she spun around and let him have it right between the legs. Henry howled and went down on his knees. He gave off a pitiful moan and crawled off into the ditch. She started after him, but I grabbed her and pointed back toward the car where Scud was getting pounded, one twin holding him from behind, the other hammering away at him.

Andie let out a yowl like an enraged mother cat and charged. The twins looked up when they heard her shriek and saw a wild woman, claws out, ready to rip their eyes from their skulls. They dropped Scud and took off running down the road.

Scud climbed painfully to his feet. He wasn't looking so good. His nose was gushing blood, he had a nasty cut above his left eye, and he was hunched over, holding his belly like he was afraid his guts would come spilling out.

"You okay?" I asked.

Scud nodded and forced himself to stand up straight. "You see that muffler come flyin' offa there?" He laughed, then coughed.

Andie said, "If you don't die, Franklin Scudder, I think I'm gonna kill you myself. I might as well just go beat my head up against the side of the barn as go out with the likes of you."

Somehow, Scud managed to grin and wink at me. "Yeah," he said. "But it's a lot more exciting."

# Hearing About Pearl

The next morning I was moving pretty slow. I felt as if every muscle in my body had been pummeled, which was exactly what had happened. Old man Murphy never said a word. He never commented about the bruise on my cheek or the cut on my chin. And he never mentioned Andie's torn dress, but the next time she wanted to go to the movies with Scud the old man just shook his head no.

He didn't care what I did, though, so long as I had my chores done, and the next time Scud stopped by, I climbed in his Ford and we drove down to Lake City to pick up a few bushels of apples from an farmer down there, and drove 'em back up to Memory to sell to the townsfolk. Scud made ten cents a bushel, and he gave me a nickel for helping.

I was getting to like him a lot. That might seem strange, since he'd got me in trouble more often than he'd got me out of it, but it was like he'd said that night he'd rolled the cherry bombs up the Gleasons' tailpipe—at least it was exciting. You never knew what he was going to do.

After the fight with the Gleasons, Scud and I were bonded like the two musketeers. It would've been three musketeers, except that Andie was grounded and besides, there was that awkwardness when the three of us were together. Scud would stop by nearly every day. I think mostly it was to see Andie, but since she was forbidden to get in his car, it was me who went driving off with him if I had my chores done. Sometimes we'd do something constructive, but more often we would just drive around and talk.

Scud did most of the talking. He wanted to be rich, and he made you believe he was going to make it happen. There was no denying that he knew how to make a buck. Eighteen years old and he was making as much with his wheeling and dealing as anybody in Memory. One week, he told me, he made fifty dollars by selling a car that wasn't even his. What he'd done was, he found a used Chrysler that a guy up in Hastings was selling for two hundred twenty dollars. Scud took it for a test-drive, drove it all the way to Lake City, and sold it to another guy for two hundred fifty dollars. Then he hitchhiked back to Hastings and told the guy who was selling the car that his car had broke down five miles out of town and wasn't worth two hundred twenty dollars. The guy was pretty upset about that, and when offered a flat two hundred dollars, according to Scud, the guy was glad to take it.

Scud lived with his mother in a little white clapboard farmhouse on the south end of Memory. Mrs. Scudder was a hollow-eyed mouse of a woman who rarely left the house. She spent her days, as near as I could tell, sewing quilts to sell and spending all the rest of her time cooking and cleaning. Their house was small, but it was the cleanest house I'd ever seen. I never asked Scud about where his father was because I didn't want to have to talk about *my* father, but one day while we were driving down toward Wabasha just to be driving someplace, he told me his dad was dead.

"That's too bad," I said.

"No it's not," Scud said. "He used to beat the hell out of me and my mom both. He was a creep. I'm glad he's dead."

I could understand that, and hearing him say it I felt like we were closer than ever.

Scud said, "I killed him, y'know." He looked at the expression on my face and gave out one of his wild, high-pitched laughs. "Naw, not really. He got drunk and took a snooze on the tracks. You couldn't tell him from a dead possum when they gathered up the parts."

All I could think to say was, "Yuk."

"I hated him," Scud said. "He was a jerk."

That same trip down to Wabasha, on the way back, Scud pulled out a folded-up sheet of newspaper from his pocket and handed it to me. "Whatdya know about this?" he asked.

I unfolded the sheet and looked it over. It was one of the financial pages from the St. Paul *Pioneer Press*—row after row of tiny writing didn't interest me a whole lot. It might just as well have been Chinese.

"What about it?" I asked.

"I found it in my car a few weeks back, just after you tried to pay off Mrs. Gleason with that phony coin."

"So?"

"So look at the date."

I looked. July 30, 1996.

As tight as Scud and I had gotten, I still hadn't told him anything about where I really came from. I hadn't told anybody, because I knew that one way or another it would get me in trouble. And as much as I liked hanging out with Scud, I didn't trust him one hundred percent. Or even ninety percent. I figured it would be a mistake to completely trust anyone who wanted to be rich as bad as Scud did.

"It must be a misprint or something," I said, remembering that I had used a newspaper to wrap a peanut butter sandwich during my second trip through the door.

"Just like that phony money you had?"

"That's right."

He took the sheet of newspaper back, folding it with one hand while he steered with the other. "You ever read a book called *The Time Machine?*"

"I've seen the movie," I said.

"Really? I didn't know they'd made a movie out of it. It never played in Red Wing, that's for sure."

"I saw it on TV," I said. I realized as soon as I'd said it that I'd made a mistake.

"Where's Teavy?" asked Scud.

"Um, it's down by Chicago."

The thing was, even though Scud suspected I was from another time, the idea was so far-fetched that he didn't really believe it. If he'd really thought it was possible, he would have known it was true. As it was, he believed it the way you might believe in, say, vampires. You suspect that they might be out there, but you don't go rubbing garlic on your neck every night. I think what Scud liked then was the idea that I might be something special, but he didn't want to scratch too hard because he didn't want to be disappointed. A little like the way I'd felt about the door. Like I wasn't sure I wanted to know if it was real.

What was most real to me then was life on the Murphys' farm. The old man kept me shoveling and baling and cutting and chopping and whatever else he could think of, and I almost never got to spend a minute alone with Andie. If it wasn't for her, I think I'd have hit the road. I'd heard from Scud that a lot of defense jobs were opening up in the Twin Cities, and guys were making over forty cents an hour.

But I stuck around. I had half a century to kill, so I figured a few more months at the Murphy place would be just a drop in the bucket.

A week or so after Thanksgiving I was splitting wood out

behind the barn, not thinking or anything, just working and enjoying the feel of it. Splitting was hard work, swinging that sixteen-pound splitting maul over and over again, driving the wedge into the big pieces, but it was work I liked—clean, hard, and satisfying. I loved the way the maul felt in my hands when it hit hard and square, and the *ka-chunk* sound of a clean-split log. And it was a beautiful day, one of those rare late autumn days with plenty of sun, no wind, and the temperature up in the fifties. I'd been at it for nearly an hour, my flannel shirt moist with sweat, when Andie came around the side of the barn with a quart Mason jar full of cool apple cider and something wrapped in a red-checked kitchen towel. I stuck the maul in a block of oak, guzzled half the cider in one swallow, and wiped my mouth on my sleeve.

Chopping wood always made me feel tough and cocky.

"Thought you might be a bit thirsty," Andie said, grinning.

"You got that right," I said. "What you got in that towel?"

"Nothing. Why?"

"On account of I smell something good."

"Maybe you're just smelling me."

"Maybe I am. You smell like banana bread."

"Why, Jack, that's one of the nicest things anybody ever said to me!"

She opened up the towel, and, of course, there was a loaf of banana bread, warm from the oven, steam still rising off it.

So we sat down on the woodpile and I used the maul to slice up the loaf and we ate and talked, just sitting in the sun and enjoying ourselves. It wasn't often that Andie and I got to be by ourselves. Old man Murphy always seemed to be just around the corner, watching us in that owly way he had.

Andie told me she wanted to travel to China someday.

"I don't want to spend my life here, where the most exciting thing around is when somebody shoves a bunch of cherry bombs up a tailpipe."

"I couldn't believe he did that."

"Yeah, well, everybody in town knows about it by now. I think Daddy even heard about it, and he don't know nothin'."

"He sure seems to know what you're doing."

Andie grinned. "He didn't know what me and Scuderoo did last night."

All of a sudden my bellyful of banana bread didn't feel so good. "Whadya mean?" I asked.

"I sneaked out last night, after you and Daddy went to bed."

"Whadya mean?" I said again. I felt awful, both because I still hadn't made peace with the idea of Andie and Scud together, and because I didn't like that I hadn't been included. Of course, whatever they'd been doing was probably something they wouldn't want me around for. Which made me feel even worse.

Andie laughed, looking right at me. It wasn't a mean laugh, and she made it less painful by reaching over and giving me a light sock on the shoulder.

"We just went for a walk," she said. "I don't get to see him no more, you know, since Daddy laid the law down. He says I'm not supposed to go out with Scud till Christmas. Only I don't think it'll be that long. Daddy's a softie at heart, you know."

"You like him a lot, don't you?"

"He's my daddy," she said.

"I mean Scud."

"Oh! I like him okay. We known each other since we was kids. He doesn't have a lot of friends, Jack. Just you and me. A lot of kids, they don't like Scud. He's sort of a wise guy."

"I know."

"It's sort of sad, though. I don't like him as much as he likes me."

“He likes you a lot.” I thought about something Scud had said to me one day. “He says he’s gonna marry you.” My voice went weak on those last two words.

Andie looked away. “I don’t know about that,” she said.

I waited for her to say more, but just then old man Murphy appeared and stood there looking at us with a sort of nothing expression on his face. Andie winked at me, then picked up the empty Mason jar and the checkered towel and walked past him without a word.

The old man looked at the wood I’d chopped and stacked. He nodded and said, “You do good work, son. Think how much wood you’d split if you’d keep your mind on it.” He turned and followed Andie back toward the house.

For the rest of that day, I couldn’t think about much other than what Andie had said. And I wondered what she’d meant by that wink.

That night after dinner the old man fell asleep listening to the radio. I went back to the kitchen to see if Andie needed help with the dishes. She was standing in the open back door.

“Come here,” she whispered, stepping out into the night.

I followed her. The air was like silk, warm and moist.

“It’s never like this in December,” she said.

It must have been close to sixty degrees outside.

“Let’s go for a walk,” she said. “We won’t get a chance to feel the air on our skin again for months.”

We headed down the driveway to the road. The moon was bright enough to cast knife-edged shadows. She took my hand, squeezed it hard.

“I like you, Jack,” she whispered. In the silence, her voice boomed in my ear. We followed our shadows, saying nothing more. We walked until we came upon a car parked by the side of the road. An old woman sat in the driver's seat, staring at us.

"Let's go back," I said.

Andie nodded. We turned and went back the way we had come. As we reached the drive leading to the farm, Andie said, "I wonder who that was?"

"Who?"

"The man in the car."

"It was an old woman," I said.

She laughed and punched me lightly on the shoulder. "You're such a kidder," she said.

The next morning the temperature dropped fifty degrees and the sky fell in. We got the first snowstorm of the season, and it was a big one. There were drifts six feet high in places, and I shoveled more snow in two days than I'd shoveled in my entire life. The worst part was, every time I complained or tried to take a break, the old man, who was shoveling away despite his bad wrist, would start talking about how this wasn't nothing compared to the big one the year before. To him, this was just a dusting. But there was so much snow that to get anyplace—like from the silo to the barn, for instance—you had to shovel your way there. The farmyard became a maze of shoveled paths—everywhere you walked you'd have a snowbank on each side so high you could hardly see over it. It took me two days to shovel the driveway out as far as the road.

After that second day of shoveling my hands were like claws and my back felt like a slab of pain. I remember dragging myself back into the house late in the afternoon just as the sun was dropping behind the trees. The old man was sitting in front of the woodstove holding his wrist in a bucket full of snow. He did that to keep it from swelling up too bad. I sat down next to him and stared into the fire.

"Bet you never got no snow like this in Chicago," he said.

"Nope."

"It'll get worse," he said.

We sat without speaking, listening to Andie clanking pans around in the kitchen. After a while, the old man spoke again. "You remember you was asking about a family named Skoro?"

My heart thumped. "Yeah?"

"Well, I was thinking that name was sorta familiar. Finally remembered where I'd heard it before. Was a Skoro family up in Hastings. At least I think that's where they was. Reason I remember is one of the Skoro gals married a fella here in town. Only she ain't named Skoro no more, a course."

So, I thought, maybe my grandfather was from Hastings, fifty miles to the north. Maybe he'd moved to Memory later on.

"You should ask your buddy Scudder about it."

"Scud? Why?"

"On account it was his momma was a Skoro. At least I think that was who she was."

Right at that moment, somebody banged on the door, then opened it and stuck his head in.

It was Scud.

"You hear? You hear?"

"Shut that dang door!" the old man shouted.

Scud quickly stepped in and closed the door. "You had your radio on?" he asked.

"Does it sound like it's on? Hear what?"

"It's the Japs," he said.

Even though I'd known it was coming, it was hard to take it in.

"They bombed us," he said. "Some place called Pearl Harbor."

# THE SECOND NOTEBOOK: THE CANAL

*The following account is based on information supplied by Sawako Tsurumi, a Japanese citizen whom I interviewed in Tokyo in 1997. According to Mrs. Tsurumi, these events occurred in July 1981.*

*A gray-haired Japanese gentleman and his wife flew into the Minneapolis–St. Paul International Airport aboard a Boeing 747. They had left Tokyo, Japan, eighteen hours earlier, and they were very tired. The woman wanted to check into a hotel immediately, but the man overrode her objections, insisting that they complete their journey that day. They rented a Ford Escort, then drove out of the airport onto the freeway. The man hunched over the wheel, staring out through his thick, bifocal glasses, staying in the right-hand lane, keeping the speedometer at a sedate forty-five miles per hour, trying to ignore his wife's chatter, straining to decipher the peculiar American road signs. He made more than one wrong turn, at one point traveling thirty-nine miles in the wrong direction.*

*It took them over four hours to drive the seventy-three miles to a small town on the western shore of Lake Pepin, where they made inquiries at the post office. The postmaster, a crabby woman who did not care for strangers, Japanese or otherwise, gruffly directed them up the bluff road to the large, gray house known locally as Boggs's End.*

*The woman who answered the door was taller than the Japanese gentlemen, but not much younger. Her hair was almost entirely gray, with only a few strands of rust remaining. She had the lined and freckled face of a woman who had spent much of her life outdoors, and her hands were rough from years of tending the gardens surrounding her home. The woman's eyes, however, remained bright and green, with the sparkle of youth.*

*In precise but heavily accented English, the Japanese gentleman introduced himself as Tadashi Tsurumi. His wife's name was Sawako.*

*Tadashi Tsurumi complimented the woman on her gardens, which were lush at that time of year. He was particularly impressed by the stand of purple, pink, and bloodred hollyhocks, a plant with which he was unfamiliar.*

*In his hands, Tadashi Tsurumi carried a small package wrapped in decorated rice paper. He offered it to the woman. Puzzled, she accepted the gift, then invited the couple in for coffee and banana bread, which she had baked just that morning. Her husband, she said, was not at home. He had driven up to Minneapolis to meet with his stockbroker.*

*Once they were settled in the kitchen, the woman opened the package. Inside was a wrinkled and stained clothbound notebook with part of the front cover missing. Many of the pages were partially or completely missing.*

*Tadashi Tsurumi explained.*

*"More than forty years ago, during the regrettable conflict between our countries, I was stationed under General*

*Kawaguchi on an island called Guadalcanal, a terrible place for both our peoples. A place not worth the life of a single dog, yet many good men died there." He clucked his tongue and reached out to touch his wife's hand. Her face remained still, betraying no emotion.*

*"My Sawako's brothers, both of them."*

*"I'm sorry," said the woman.*

*"It was many years ago. It is not something we think about every day. In our histories it is called The Isle of Death."*

*The woman nodded.*

*Tadashi went on. "I was one of the few of my people to leave the island alive. It was a great defeat for us. A terrible time. Sometimes, in my sleep, I am back in that jungle with the rats and the insects—what do you call them? The small ones that suck your blood?"*

*"Mosquitoes."*

*"Yes. They were everywhere, like fog. But excuse me, please, I am telling you about this notebook. You see, like many young men, I was very proud to be fighting for my emperor. I wished to bring back—how do you say it? Remembrances?"*

*"Souvenirs?"*

*"Yes, souvenirs. One morning my group, my squad, we were fighting very hard against a—a machine gun. Deep in the jungle, where no one should be, death spitted out at us through the leaves. Up in the rocks, very protected, it spitted death. Many of us died, over twenty. I myself was injured. It took many bullets and bombs—mortars—before we were able to destroy it. The American who had attacked us, only one! He died. A bad day for all. Yes, this is when I found this notebook. The lone machine gunner, he died a great hero for your people. Many of my friends died also.*

*There was death everywhere in the jungle that day. The men died and the rats feasted."*

*Tadashi Tsurumi continued. "For many years I have kept this notebook. But I am no longer this young man who collects the memories of dead heroes. I have known for years that the right thing to do was to return his words to his family, to those who respect his memory. Sawako and I, we have always wished to come to America, and now we are here, and I am returning the notebook to you, as he would wish. He has written this place and this town name on the inside cover, you see, and so we have found you."*

*The woman opened the tattered cover of the notebook and read a few words. She looked up, her green eyes suddenly welling with tears. "He was killed?"*

*"As I say, the bullets and mortar shells rained down. He was only one man. The machine gun fell silent. When we reached the rocks that had concealed him, the man was dead, and I found this." He touched the notebook reverently. "I have returned it to you, now we must go."*

*The woman's face was slick with tears, but she forced a smile and said, "Won't you stay for lunch?"*

*Tadashi Tsurumi stood and bowed. "We thank you, but we must drive back to the Twin Cities of Minneapolis and St. Paul. We have tickets to see your great Minnesota Twins play the Yankees of New York."*

*The two visitors bowed again and left.*

*The woman stared down at the open notebook, then began to read.*

*The original eight-by-ten-inch clothbound notebook was in extremely poor condition. Many of the pages were missing, partially missing, or unreadable due to bloodstains, water damage, or illegible handwriting. I have not attempted to fill in the gaps in the writer's narrative. What you are about to read is an accurate transcription of the notebook kept by Jack Lund, Cpl., U.S.M.C.*

*—P. H.*

U.S. Navy Transport *Alexander*
Somewhere in the middle of nowhere
July 30, 1942

Dear Andie,

They got us packed in here like sardines. The only way a guy can get a breath of air that doesn't smell like some other guy's sweat or vomit or worse is to sneak up on deck after lights out and find a spot on the leeward side of this rust bucket they call a ship. It's the middle of the night right now and they don't want us to show any lights, so I'm under a canvas with a flashlight, leaning up against one of the big guns.

The waves are as high as a house. About three quarters of the guys are seasick. As I write this, I can hear somebody a few yards away from me puking out over the rail. It's night now, but in the day you can see these schools of little silver fish that follow the ship. I think they live on the half-digested remains of our dinners, only they seem to enjoy it more.

I'm one of the lucky ones who isn't bothered by the waves. But it will sure feel good to walk on solid ground. They've finally told us where we are headed—some place called the Solomon Islands, wherever that is. Scud thinks it will be like paradise, with coconuts and native girls in grass skirts! Only somehow I don't think so and even if I do see a girl in a grass skirt, I'm sure she won't be nothing compared to you. I miss you a lot.

Probably you'll never read this, but it feels good to be writing anyway. Maybe someday I'll get a chance to send it. I can't believe how far away from Memory I've traveled. I wish sometimes I'd never let Scud talk me into joining up. I could be working with you in the munitions plant. We could see each other every day. This isn't my war anyways. But of course you wouldn't have respected that, would you, Andie? Even though I know we're going to win this war, anyway, and nothing I do or don't do is going to change that. No matter what happens to me.

Scud talks about you a lot. I have to tell you, Andie, I feel like a rat sometimes.

Love,
Jack

P.S. Today is my seventeenth birthday. Happy birthday to me.

U.S. Navy Transport *Alexander*
August 12, 1942

Dear Andie,

This ocean is so big, and we've been on it for so long, I've almost forgotten what it feels like to stand on a surface that is not constantly moving. Even when the sea is dead calm, the deck vibrates and echoes with the turning of the engines. The propellers that drive this ship are as wide as your corncrib is high.

We're getting pretty itchy after two weeks at sea. There's not much to do here except try to stay out of the way and try not to think about what is to come. Our platoon leader, a guy named Williams who is all of twenty-three, tells us in no uncertain terms that some of us aren't going to make it back. Most of the guys on board don't believe him, but I do. I don't remember much about what happened in the South Pacific, but I do know that a lot of soldiers died. I'm starting to wonder if it was such a good idea to lie about my age and join the Marines. What's done is done, I guess.

Scud has been killing time by playing in the poker game that seems to be going on twenty-four hours a day. So far he's lost all his money and most of mine. I don't mind, though, since I figure we're either going to make it back, or not. How much cash I've got in my pocket won't make a bit of difference.

I'll never forget what you said to me that day last February, the day I told you that Scud and I had signed up with the Marines.

You said, "Don't die, Jack. I want you to come back."

I said, "Don't worry. Me and Scud, we'll be back."

I remember we were standing in the kitchen. You said, "You just make sure you come back." You pressed your palm against my chest. You said, "Scud will take care of himself. It's all he cares about."

That was the first time I knew I had a chance with you. I'd always thought you were Scud's girl, the way he talked about you, the way you let him talk. Then you clasped my hand in yours. You had been washing dishes, your hand was red and hot with little soap bubbles still on your knuckles. You pulled my hand to your breast, and then you kissed me, your father sitting in his chair just around the corner not ten feet away. If I close my eyes I can still feel your breast beneath my hand, your lips touching mine.

Andie, the feeling I get, remembering those last weeks with you, it's like it hurts but at the same time it feels so good.

I still think we should have told Scud. You said it wouldn't be right to send him off to war that way, but like you said, Scud can take care of himself. What about me? I'm the one who has to live a lie, listening to him tell all the guys about this great gal he has back home, winking at me, and me not able to say a word.

There I go again, feeling sorry for myself.

Love,
Jack

U.S. Navy Transport *Alexander*
August 15, 1942

Dear Andie,

Remember last winter just before we shipped out, that day we stayed up late with your father drinking his home brew, and he fell asleep, and we were talking and I told you I was from the future. I keep wondering, did you believe me? Or were you just being polite? I've told almost nothing about my history because, frankly, I was afraid you'd think me insane. And I wouldn't blame you.

I'm lying on my bunk. I can feel the engines.

If you had told me you were from the future, maybe *I* wouldn't have believed *you*.

I guess it doesn't matter. I know it's true. The door is there. When I get back I'll show it to you. It's in the closet of the small bedroom on the third floor of Boggs's End. Actually, there are two doors. You have to go through the door in the closet and down a flight of stairs to get to the door that really matters: The fifty-year door, as Mr. Boggs called it. The door is made of metal, and it is very cold. It used to be that you could go through the door from the outside, too. That would take you into the future. But that's impossible now, since I carried out my promise to Mr. Boggs. I suppose this doesn't make any sense to you. What difference does it make? I won't be sending this letter, anyway.

Here comes Scud.

(Later) Scud is curious about this notebook. He wants to know what I can find to write about. Of course, I'll never let him see it. I can't imagine what he'd do if he knew about you and me. I wish we'd just told him. Oh well. It's something we can deal with when we get back.

I must be feeling pretty guilty, because I just loaned him my last fifteen bucks, even though I know he's going to lose every last dime.

Love,
Jack

U.S. Navy Transport *Alexander*
Somewhere in the South Pacific
August 16, 1942

Dear Andie,

Do you have secrets, too? I have been sitting thinking about all the things I haven't told you, and I wonder whether there are things you haven't told me. Are you really who you say you are? Or are you a being from another planet? Or an angel come to Earth to torment me by being in my heart, yet thousands of miles away?

This voyage is making me crazy. Sometimes I wonder whether all the things I think have happened to me were real, or just a waking dream. When we were in boot camp the guys used to talk about what you'd have to do to get a Section Eight. That's what they call it when one of the army docs signs a paper that says you're too crazy to be sent out into the jungle to die. Some guys say the only way you could get a Section Eight would be by trying to kill yourself, but I think if I just talked about what really happened to me, they'd have me in a straitjacket faster than you can say "time travel."

But the fact is, Andie, I was born in 1979. At least, I think I was. Sometime maybe I'll tell you all about it. About how my grandfather Skoro tried to kill me, but he was the one who died. And about my parents. Let me tell you about my mother—

*(pages missing)*

—how I decided to go back through the door. I'll be an old man by then, but I have to try to change things. Do you think I'm crazy now? Well, if you don't, it's probably because I haven't told you about the Boggses.

I always wondered what would happen if I went through the door again, when I was already in the past. I mean, if I went back into the house and climbed up to the third floor and went back through the closet door, down the staircase, and out through the cold metal door. Would I go even farther back in time? And what if I stepped out into a time before the house had been built? Would I be able to return?

The week before Scud and I got on the bus to Fort Snelling, I decided to find out. I walked over to Boggs's End and pulled the boards off a window and climbed inside. Talk about creepy. It was daylight outside, a crisp, sunny February day, but inside the house was dark because of all the boarded-up windows. Every step I took sent up a cloud of dust.

I climbed the stairs to the third floor and went to the closet and, sure enough, there was the door. I went down the steps to the metal door. I sat there in the dark for a long time before turning the knob and pulling the door open and stepping out into the summer sun.

I'm trying to remember the first thing that hit me. I think it was the clouds. I was looking out over the edge of the bluff. Above, the sky was hazy blue, with the sun hammering down, the air hot and thick with moisture. But out across the river, a huge thunderhead rose up so high I had to tip my head back to see it. I heard thunder, faint and far. Pillars of rain fell from the cloud onto the far shore and lightning flickered on the Wisconsin bluffs, yet I could feel the sun on my shoulders.

I heard children's voices.

Two little black-haired girls in white dresses were playing with a baby goat. One of the girls was wearing a bonnet. Have you ever even *seen* a bonnet except in fairy tale books? The other girl had tied her bonnet onto the baby goat's head. The goat chewed on the string. The lawn was bright green, the grass cropped. Two full-grown goats rested in the shade of an oak tree. I turned and looked back at the house. The vines I remembered were gone, replaced by a bed of hollyhocks. The white paint was new. The metal door shone like a mirror. I started toward the edge of the bluff to look down on the town, but was distracted by cries from the two girls. They had seen me. The baby goat trotted toward me. The girls turned and ran back around the house. I thought about going back through the door, but I still hadn't learned where I was. I continued toward the edge. The town came into view. At first, everything looked normal. I might have been in 1942, or in 1994, or anywhere in between. Then I noticed that there were no cars. There were wagons, and a buggy, and horses.

"Good day!" said a deep, booming voice.

A tall, black-bearded, shirtless man in gray overalls and a wide-brimmed straw hat stood a few yards behind me.

I said, "Hello."

He stared at me, his ruddy face motionless, arms crossed, big, rough hands resting on thick biceps. Behind him, standing at the corner of the house, a small woman in a black dress held a baby to her chest. The two girls peeked out from behind her, their dark eyes staring at me with a mixture of fear and wonder. The man shifted his feet, and for a moment I thought he was going to rush at me and fling me over the precipice. But suddenly he smiled, showing a set of brilliantly white, perfectly ordered teeth.

"Would you care for a glass of lemonade?" he asked—

*(The bottom half of this page is charred and for the most part illegible.)*

—of the little girls crawling around under the picnic table.

Mrs. Boggs, who never uttered a word the whole time I was there, busied herself by making sure our glasses were replenished, offering us more plums, cookies, and apple wedges, and shaking her fingers at her daughters whenever they threatened to misbehave, which was more or less all the time.

Mr. Boggs, unlike his squirmy offspring, wasted no motion. When he chose to move his large body, his actions were considered and precise. For instance, when he took a swallow of lemonade, he lifted the glass to his mouth with a single motion, and poured its contents down his throat. Only his eyes remained in constant motion. As near as I could tell, they missed nothing—

*(missing page)*

—about the door," he said.

I did want to know, but I'd avoided asking.

"It must have been a considerable shock for you, young man. You must have come from . . . what? About nineteen thirty-seven?"

"Nineteen forty-two," I said.

Mr. Boggs laughed. "About what you'd expect from a fifty-year door," he said. "They never were worth the metal they're made of. Sloppy, very sloppy. So, you must be having that war right about then, eh?"

I nodded. "What do you mean about the door?" I asked.

"It's a fifty-year door, young man. Only it doesn't hold to spec. Shoddy manufacturing. You never know when you're headed for."

I struggled to make sense of what he was saying.

"You mean if I go back, I might wind up some different place?"

Mr. Boggs thought that was really funny. Even Mrs. Boggs smiled.

He finally said, "Don't worry about it, son. You always go back to where you came from, it's just that you can't know for sure where you've been—

*(illegible)*

—you understand?"

I didn't. I was still trying to deal with the idea of being back in 1887. What Mr. Boggs was asking me to do seemed reasonable, and I had agreed to do it, but I didn't think I'd ever understand.

He shook his head sadly. "You don't understand, do you, son?"

I shook my head.

"But you'll do as I ask?"

"I'll do it." The texture of the air had changed from warm to clammy. The storm moved across the lake.

"You know, you never told me when you were from."

"Nineteen forty-two."

"I mean before that."

"I was born in nineteen seventy-nine." The thundercloud's leading edge eclipsed the sun.

"Hmmph!" He crossed his arms and lowered his thick black eyebrows. "I suppose you know that when you do as I ask, you'll be stuck. You won't be able to return to the nineteen nineties."

Lightning flashed.

"Yes, I will."

"Oh?" He seemed amused. "How?"

"I'll age," I said.

Mr. Boggs's eyes widened. Then he began to chuckle, the deep sound of his laughter joined by thunder—

*(Several pages here were missing, torn, or obscured by brown stains.)*

Henderson Field
Guadalcanal
August 18, 1942

Dear Andie,

The scaredest I've ever been was when we went over the side of the ship, climbed down those cargo nets, and rode the landing craft up onto the beach. They told us the beachhead was secure—the first landings were twelve days ago—but Jap snipers were shooting at us from the moment we hit shore, but not one of our guys got killed. A fellow from Mississippi named Atkins took one in the knee. Lucky guy. He gets a free ride back to Pearl.

Remember I said we might land on some tropical paradise? Well, you can forget about that. The name of this island is Guadalcanal. Nobody seems to know what that means. There are no canals here, but the guys have all started calling it "The Canal." What there is, is mosquitoes and biting flies and spiders the size of crabs and crabs the size of cats. The beaches are all right to look at, but between the bugs and the snipers, I wouldn't want to do any sunning there. About twenty yards in from the water's edge at high tide you run into this kunai grass that stands maybe seven feet tall and has edges like a bread knife. The stuff is almost impenetrable, and there's about a hundred feet of it between the beach and the jungle, which I haven't been in yet but I hear it's even worse—

*(illegible)*

—sitting in the tent that serves as our mess hall, looking out over the muddy, shell-holed airstrip we now call Henderson Field, which was the first thing we took away from the Japs.

Nobody else is here right now, since it's way past dinnertime. It's a good place to be alone, and with close to twenty thousand of us here, that's not easy.

God, do I miss you.

Love,
Jack

Henderson Field
Guadalcanal
September 2, 1942

Dear Andie,

We are all waiting for Washing Machine Charlie. There's no point in trying to sleep until he's come and gone. He comes every night, sometimes early, sometimes late. You can hear him a long way off and it's true, he sounds like a washing machine: *chuffa-chuffa-chuffa.*

Washing Machine Charlie is a Jap night bomber.

Imagine you are lying in your tent, sweating buckets, slapping mosquitoes, hungry as you've ever been. Most of the supplies were lost in the landings, and you've been living on rice left behind by the Japs. You are waiting. Sometimes he comes early; other times you wait till five in the morning to hear the sound of a distant washing machine. *Shuh-shuh-shuh.* The sound gets louder: *chuffa-chuffa-chuffa.* You close your eyes and grit your teeth and then you hear the explosions. *Boom. Boom. Boom.*

They are small bombs, thrown by hand from Charlie's small plane. Most nights no one is hurt, and after Charlie has left, you can sleep. Scud says that's the whole point. Charlie wants us to lose sleep waiting for him.

But Charlie's nothing compared to Tojo Time. Tojo Time is what we call the daily Jap bomber raids on the airfield. A black flag goes up from the pagoda in the middle of the airfield. Seconds later, you can hear the fluttering drone of their approach—sometimes as many as twenty bombers. As soon as they are in sight, all hell breaks loose. The antiaircraft guns start firing and everybody else heads for the slit trenches and foxholes. Then you hear, even through the antiaircraft fire, the *shhhhh* sound of falling bombs. The bombs hit with a *whump*

*whump whump,* like a giant's exploding footsteps. *Whump whump whump.* Six to eight big steps from each bomber, and if you are one of the unlucky ones, the giant will stomp you flat in your tent.

After they leave, the dead are counted, the wounded are treated, and the rest of us start filling in the craters in the airfield.

Other than that, we are all bored. Our platoon, which is attached to Colonel Edson's B Company, will be hitting the jungle again tomorrow. There're all kinds of rumors about a big Jap force building up out in the jungle, and maybe it's true. Most of the information that gets filtered down through the ranks is bull, but you never know. This will be the third time our platoon has been out, and in a way I'm looking forward to it. It's either that, or wait for the malaria to get you. Almost a quarter of the guys in our platoon have got the bug. What malaria does is, you get the sweats, then a few hours later you get the chills, then you get the sweats again. At first, they say, it's not so bad, but after a few cycles it wears you out and it's all you can do to lift a glass of water. Most of those who got it can handle it, but four of us are in the hospital and Simmons has actually died of it. That leaves only eighteen of our platoon in fighting shape, and we landed on this pesthole with twenty-nine.

Flanagan, Mrosak, and Hoff were all killed on the airfield when they were helping mount a bomb on one of the P-400s and somebody screwed up. Desimone tripped over a mine the first time we went out on patrol. Billig got appendicitis. They say he's going to be okay. And Sergeant Sadowski, he got stomped by the giant.

And I still haven't seen a single Japanese on the ground. I haven't even shot my gun yet.

By the way, after Sarge Sadowski got stomped, Scud got

himself a field promotion. It's Sergeant Scudder now, and you better remember it. He's still the same Scud when it's just him and me together, but when anybody else is around he treats me like his favorite dog.

Love,
Jack

P.S. I got a promotion, too. It's Corporal Lund now. But you can call me Jack.

Henderson Field
September 10, 1942

Dear Andie,

I got a bad feeling. I got a feeling I'm going to die. I haven't even been born yet, and here I'm about to die. I should be worrying about my mother. If I die, I won't be able to save her. But all I can think about is you.

You know that rumor about the Japs coming at us through the jungle? Well, it's official now. They're out there and they're coming this way. Colonel Edson has told us we're to secure a ridge about a mile south of the airfield. What that means is that the Japs are going to have to go right through us to get to the airfield. I don't know what's going to happen, Andie, but I got a feeling it's gonna be bad.

(Later) Now I got an even worse feeling. I just got back from a "dinner" that was nothing more than a scoop of rice, a bowl of piss-yellow bouillon, and a cup of something—I couldn't tell if it was supposed to be coffee, tea, or dishwater. Anyway, I was walking back to the ghetto (which is what we call our little tent city way on the other side of the airstrip) holding a piece of canvas over my head to keep the rain from running down my back, when I saw somebody crawl out of my tent. I was a ways off, and it was hard to see through the rain, but I think it was Scud.

That's one thing you aren't supposed to do. Go in somebody's tent.

Andie, I think he was looking at this notebook.

I've been trying to get up the nerve to go talk to him. We're heading out into the jungle.

I guess it's now or never.

*(Unlike the previous entries, which were inscribed with a*

*blue fountain pen, the final pages of the notebook are written in pencil. Many of the words are smeared and difficult or impossible to decipher.)*

Well, I was right. Dead right. I'm going to die, Andie. For all practical purposes, I'm dead already. My right eye is swollen shut, or maybe gone. I don't know, when I touch it, it hurts so bad I can't tell what's left there. I'm all alone, except for the dead man at my feet and about fifty Japanese soldiers camped a few hundred yards upwind of my position. It's only a matter of time before they notice the cave, before they find me.

I was right about Scud, too. He read the notebook. He didn't admit it, of course—when I accused him he gave me his "what, are you nuts?" look.

"Then what were you doing in my tent?" I asked him.

"I wasn't in your damn tent, Corporal," he said.

I wondered how much he'd had a chance to read—

*(illegible)*

—moved us out two hours before dawn. The ridge we were supposed to secure was about a mile inland from Henderson Field, and our platoon was to occupy a little knob of rock another quarter mile beyond the ridge. There was supposed to be a sort of trail leading from the airfield to the ridge, but the mud got so bad that Lieutenant Cole decided we'd be better off cutting straight through the jungle, climbing over the waist-high roots and using our bayonets to hack our way through walls of vines and patches of kunai grass.

You'd think a mile isn't all that far to walk, but in the dark, trying to get through the tangle of roots, vines, saw-toothed grass, and sinkholes, carrying forty-pound packs and enough guns, mortars, grenades, and ammo to destroy half the Japanese army, we'd be lucky to make five hundred yards an hour. That's assuming nothing goes wrong.

Twenty minutes into the jungle, Jesperson, a big tall kid from Arkansas, had twisted his ankle so bad the lieutenant told him to try to make it back to the base. There wasn't much else we could do, since Colonel Edson was counting on us being in position by 0700. Then it started to rain.

By the time the blackness gave way to dreary, rain-streaked gray, we were a mess, totally soaked, muddy, cut up from the grass, and insect-bit everywhere a bit of skin showed. Being able to see made the going easier, though, and by 0700 we had reached our position and dug in.

The knob stuck up out of the jungle like a big, grassy pimple erupting from a sea of deep green treetops. We could see Edson's Ridge just to the northwest, where A Company was digging in. Our platoon was supposed to discourage the Japanese from skirting the ridge on the east. The jungle canopy was so dense they coulda walked right between our position and the ridge and we'd never have known it, but what do I know about military strategy?

I was cleaning the mud from the barrel of my Springfield when the first artillery rounds fell, not two hundred yards in front of us.

And those were from our side.

The artillery barrage went on for twenty minutes. When it finally stopped and I stuck my head up out of my shallow foxhole, the solid green mass of trees appeared to be untouched, but for a cloud of blue smoke rising through the fronds.

Then we waited, watching the furtive movements of A Company taking their positions on Edson's Ridge. The other guy in the foxhole with me was Freddy Seberg, a nice guy, but not very bright. He had a habit of asking stupid questions, then answering them himself.

"What's all that smoke? I guess it's from the shells, huh."

I said, "Yeah." That was about all you ever had to say around Freddy. There was really no point in even listening when he talked.

I guess I shouldn't be speaking ill of the dead—

*(illegible)*

—shots from the ridge, all of a sudden it was like a million firecrackers going off. All of us that were in a position to watch had our heads up out of our holes trying to see what was going on, but all we could see was smoke from mortar rounds. Now and then we could hear faint screams—

*(illegible)*

—looking downslope, when Freddy said, "Is that a Jap? Yup, it's a Jap, hu-UH!"

That was the last thing he ever said. Freddy didn't have a mouth to talk with anymore. His jaw was blown clean off.

I'd never seen a man shot before, Andie, but it was nothing compared to what I'd be seeing—

*(illegible)*

—in waves, screaming Japanese, throwing grenades. Then they were on us. One of them came right over me and I fired. He didn't even see me, probably never knew what hit him. The one right behind him turned his rifle on me, I slashed at his arm with my bayonet, then stabbed. These Japanese, you get up close to one and you realize how little they are, but they got a lot of blood in them. Everything from then on was a blur. I was in a universe of blood and death and Japs, shooting and stabbing like some kind of insane killing machine. I remember Lieutenant Cole shouting for us to retreat down the back side of the knob. I looked, and saw a mortar round lift him right up into the air. I didn't need any more encouragement, I was up out of my hole and running like I've never run before, hearing the zipzip of bullets inches from my head, flying down the side of that knob, my feet hitting maybe every twenty feet, diving for the tangled protection of the jungle like it was God's arms—

*(illegible)*

—just keep going," Scud said, giving me a shove in the back.

Our BAR man, Adamson, a few feet ahead of me, fell headlong onto a rotting log. Brown beetles the size of mice scurried out, making clicking sounds with their wings. A few of them took flight, weaving through the pouring rain like a squadron of drunken, flying tanks. I watched one of them fly smack into a palm trunk, slide down into the undergrowth.

"Get that man up!" Scud ordered.

I was trying to, but it wasn't easy with Adamson all mud-slimed and tangled up in his weaponry, and weighing close to two hundred fifty pounds to boot. Each platoon had a BAR. That's a Browning Automatic Rifle, which is like a cross between a rifle and a machine gun. Because they were so heavy and awkward, it was usually given to the biggest man in the platoon. Incredibly, during that wild run off the knob and into the jungle, Adamson had held onto that BAR, bipod and all, along with six ammo boxes. I'd barely managed to hang on to my Springfield. Even more impressive was that Adamson had a hole in his gut, a few inches to the left of his navel.

The front of his shirt was soaked red, but it didn't seem to bother him. That was Adamson, farm boy from Nebraska, dumb as a cow, strong as an ox, and stubborn as a mule.

Scud came alongside, grabbed Adamson's other arm, and we lifted the Nebraskan onto his feet. Once he was upright, Scud got right in his face.

"Leave it," he said.

Adamson looked at Scud with an astonished expression on his face. "What's that?" he asked.

"Leave the damn gun and ammo. You're slowing us up, soldier."

Adamson, who had served alongside Scud as an equal for six weeks before Scud had gotten his promotion, didn't like being talked to that way. "Uh-uh," he said. *"Sir."*

Scud got so red in the face I thought he was going bust Adamson one, but he managed to swallow it.

"Look," he said, his voice strained, "if we're gonna get out of this mess, we gotta make some time."

Adamson shook his head slowly. "We don't even know where we are."

That was true. As far as we knew we were the only survivors from our platoon, and we were as lost as you can get. The fact that we'd stumbled across each other in the jungle—I'd damn near shot Scud when I first saw him—was only slightly more amazing than the fact that we were alive. At least for the time being. We could hear the muffled sound of mortar fire, but had no idea how far we'd come or in what direction. We'd been walking, if you could call it that, for hours.

"We're gonna get out," Scud said.

"Well, I ain't leaving Rudy," Adamson said. Rudy was the name he'd given to his BAR. It was also, he told me once, the name of his dog—

*(page missing)*

—obvious to me that we'd headed off in the wrong direction, but Scud wouldn't admit it.

"It's an *island,*" he said. "There is no wrong direction."

"This island's ninety miles long," I pointed out.

"Yeah, well, we'd be out a here by now wasn't for Adamson."

I looked back at the Nebraskan, who was trailing us by ten yards, still carrying the BAR and the pack full of ammo, muttering to himself. Adamson had been losing blood steadily, but he refused to stay put while we went for help. It might not have been so dumb, since the odds are we'd never have been able to find him—

*(illegible)*

—collapsed right at the base of the rocky outcropping. His eyes were open, but only the whites were visible. I shouted for Scud. I could barely make out his gray shape through the thickening rain, then I lost sight of him. I yelled again, staring at the spot where he'd disappeared into the tangled vegetation. Nothing. He was gone.

Now, I'm no hero, Andie. All the heroes I knew died back on the knob. And I might've run after Scud, leaving Adamson behind, but just then the damned Nebraskan's eyes snapped back into focus and he opened his mouth.

"Rudy?" he said. "That you, boy?"

His eyes darted around, then fixed on me, and he smiled. "Good boy," he said, then his eyes rolled up again.

I managed to drag him out of the muck up onto the mossy boulders at the base of the rock formation. The outcropping jutted up about twenty feet from the jungle floor, and was about a hundred feet across. I could see, a few yards farther up the rubble-strewn slope, what looked like a cave. There was no doubt in my mind that the Nebraskan was dying, but I couldn't just leave him on that rotting jungle floor for the rats and the beetles. I had to get him out of the rain. A man should die dry, I thought, though I now wonder what difference it makes how wet you are when you die. I'm pretty dry right now, but I don't feel any better about dying.

I stripped off Adamson's gear, including his precious Rudy and the pack full of ammo boxes. I'd dragged him halfway up to the cave when a shadow detached itself from the jungle and plodded up the slope after us.

It was Scud. I hadn't been so glad to see him since the time the Gleasons chased me up the bluff road.

Scud slung the BAR over his shoulder, grabbed the ammo pack with one hand, and Adamson's right arm with the other. The two of us had Adamson up that slope in no time. The cave was only about ten feet deep, not much more than a hollow beneath a projecting shelf of rock, but it was dry, and for the first time since we'd entered the jungle back at Henderson field, I didn't hear the sound of rain falling on my helmet. We—

*(illegible)*

—woke up with a start, sat up, and grabbed my rifle. Something had jarred me from my dream, a beautiful dream but I don't remember it. I focused on Scud, who was on his belly at the mouth of the shelter looking down the barrel of the BAR.

"What's going on?" I asked. He cut me off with a hand motion. I listened. Faint Japanese voices. Scud crawled backward.

"Can't see 'em," he said. "Passing by, maybe a hundred yards that way—" He pointed.

"They know we're here?"

"If they knew, we'd know it. By the way, Adamson's dead." He said it the way you'd tell a guy his fly is open. I looked over at Adamson and of course it was true, he was quite dead. The flies were already clustered at his closed eyelids, waiting for the dead flesh to contract and give them access.

I don't know why I'm writing this. No one will ever read it, unless some Jap picks it up off my dead body. Is that you, Jap? Well you can take this notebook and shove it. You bastards are going to lose this war, anyways, I know, because I've seen the future. Let me ask you something, Jap. Do the words "atom bomb" mean anything to you? I'm—

*(illegible due to deliberate pencil marks)*

I think I'm getting delirious, Andie. All my life, until I got to this nightmare island, I thought of the Japanese as people who made nice cars and cameras. Now I think of them as vicious, evil beasts. That can't be right, can it? I mean, they're just a bunch of scared kids like me who wish they were back home. But how can you like someone who is trying to kill you?

Where was I? Oh, yeah. Scud. So Scud looks at his watch and says to me, "It's gonna be dark in another couple hours."

"Is that good or bad?" I asked.

Scud shrugged. "They're moving away from us."

Then I noticed that the top flap of my pack was open. The piece of oilcloth I'd used to wrap this notebook lay on the rocks beside it. I looked around the shallow cave. There was my notebook, thrown up against the back wall.

Scud watched me make this discovery, his lips frozen into a hard, humorless smile.

"I had to have another look," he said. "Couldn't believe my eyes the first time I read it. My good friend Jack." He shook his head.

I didn't reply. What could I say?

"You know you ain't never going to see her again," he said.

"We might make it," I said.

Scud held his terrible smile, then crawled back to the lip and lay on his belly, staring out into the jungle for what might have been sixty seconds, though it seemed like days. I could no longer hear the sound of voices. I came up beside him and stared into the foliage, trying to make sense of it, but my eyes couldn't sort out the green scrambled mess. My mind was all knotted around Scud and you, Andie. I was in the middle of an island in the South Pacific, surrounded by Japanese soldiers, and all I could think about was Memory, Minnesota.

Is that stupid, or what?

"So what do you want to do?" I asked.

Scud turned his head and regarded me with what looked like distaste.

"I mean," I said, "do you want to stay here the night, or move out now?"

Scud moved his head slowly back and forth, as though marveling at my stupidity.

"I think we should move out now," I said. "It's obvious we're near some sort of Jap supply trail. It's only a matter of time before another bunch comes by and decides to check out this pile of rocks."

Scud said, "You can do what you want."

I left my Springfield at the entrance and moved toward the back of the cave to get my gear. Something struck me on the back of the head. My face hit the rock floor of the cavern. I twisted away, instinctively bringing my hands up in front of my face, thinking that this was it, the Japs were on us, but it wasn't the Japs.

It was Scud. I saw his face, Andie, and my entire body went numb with horror. His lips pulled back from his teeth like a vicious dog, swinging his rifle like a club, slashing at me, keeping me off balance. It was not the Scud we know, Andie. I got one hand on a rock and threw it, hit him on the jaw. He dropped his rifle and staggered back, his cheek slick with red blood. I scrabbled across the rocks, trying to get to his rifle, but he was on me again, on my back, pounding the side of my head with his fist.

All the time we were fighting, neither of us made a sound. On some level we both knew that outside our little arena the jungle was listening, full of Japanese soldiers. Had it not been for that, I'm sure he'd have just shot me.

Maybe I'd've been better off that way.

His fist kept driving into my ear, I couldn't get him off. Somehow, I got my feet under me and stood up, slamming him against the low ceiling of the cave. He fell, flat on his back, his head bouncing off a rock.

For a moment, neither of us moved. I was gasping for breath, trying to understand what had happened. Scud appeared to be out cold. I stepped over him to get his rifle, to make sure it was out of his reach. When he woke up, I wanted to be able to talk to him, and I figured it would be easier if only one of us had a gun. I wanted to explain to him about you and me, try to get him to understand that it was just something that *happened.*

I never got the chance. He wasn't out cold at all. As I stepped over him, his boot came up hard and caught me right in the crotch. I went down like a sack of grain, doubled over, my eyes squeezed shut. I opened them just in time to see that rifle butt coming at me. I didn't feel it hit, but I heard the bones in my face snap—and that's all I remember.

When I woke up it was pitch black, and I could hear the Japanese voices again. I knew, without being able to see, that Scud was gone. I lay in the dark for hours, Andie, with no company but the sound of incomprehensible voices filtering through rain, the pounding pain in my head, and the sweet, awful smell of Adamson's rapidly decaying body.

With the first light of morning, I dragged myself over to Adamson's BAR at the mouth of the cave. It may be that Scud left it for me to give me a tiny chance at survival, but I think it more likely that he simply thought me dead and didn't want to carry it. I've got myself set up here with the gun, a half-full canteen, and this notebook.

The Japs have set up some sort of camp, I would guess about three hundred yards away. I can hear them, and I can smell something cooking. Sooner or later, they'll be here, Andie, and I'm going to kill as many of them as I can, but I'm going to die. I wish I could just explain to them that this isn't my war. Their war is lost, and they should all go home. We should all go home.

I don't think they'd listen.

One other thing. I mentioned that when I saw Scud's face, when we were fighting, it wasn't the Scud we know. I meant that literally. I don't understand it, and I don't see how it could be possible, but what I saw was not Scud.

It was my grandfather's face.

Here they come.

# THE THIRD NOTEBOOK: MR. WAS

*The following documents were found in a file folder glued to the inside front cover of a soiled, mustard-colored, clothbound three-ring binder.*

—*P. H.*

r-82399
From: LAZLO C. GROTH
To: FILE
Subject: Patient MZ-54764-8
Date: 8/12/43

The subject was first observed on March 21, 1943, on the island of Guadalcanal in the Solomon Islands, raiding the garbage dump of a U.S.M.C. outpost near Henderson Field. He was naked, apparently searching for food. Because his skin had darkened from weeks or months of exposure to the sun, and because his face was severely disfigured, he was not recognized by base personnel as an American.

When challenged by guards, the subject fled. Several shots were fired, but the subject escaped into the jungle.

Six days later, on March 27, the subject was spotted again, this time by a platoon patrolling outside the perimeter of the base. After an extended pursuit, he was captured uninjured and delivered to the base hospital, where he was examined by Captain Zachary Pierssen, M.D.

According to Cpt. Pierssen's report, the subject appeared to be in a state of extreme dehydration. He had a damaged right eye socket, which had become maggot-infested. One arm had been broken and had healed at a peculiar angle. The fingers and palms of both hands were scarified, possibly from contact with hot metal, making fingerprints impossible to obtain. (Captain Pierssen noted that he had observed similar injuries on soldiers who had gripped the hot barrel of a machine gun for extended periods of time.) Several of the subject's teeth were missing. He was delirious and unable to form sentences or understand simple verbal commands. Although the subject is believed to be one of the Guadalcanal MIAs, base personnel were unable to match him with any of the missing soldiers (MIA list attached).

After being hydrated, fed, and treated for his wounds, the subject quickly gained his physical vitality, but remained irrational. He was observed on several occasions calling for his mother. When asked who his mother was, he responded by screaming repeatedly. The severity and frequency of the patient's outbursts has since abated, but Captain Pierssen recommends the use of restraints during examinations and transfers.

On August 4, 1943, Patient MZ-54764-8 was transferred here, to Pearl Harbor Naval Hospital.

(signed)
Captain Lazlo C. Groth, MC USA
Chief Psychiatry Service
Pearl Harbor

r-82399
From: LAZLO C. GROTH
To: FILE
Subject: Patient MZ-54764-8
Date: 8/19/43

During the initial examination, the patient remained in a rigid sitting posture, staring straight ahead. He was unresponsive to my questions, and as near as I could tell was utterly unaware of his surroundings. How much of this is due to his injuries and how much is a result of the high dosage of chloral hydrate he had been given remains uncertain. Although the patient appears to be passive, I have followed Captain Pierssen's recommendation and kept him in a straitjacket. At one point I was sitting behind my desk reviewing Captain Pierssen's notes when the patient suddenly spoke:

Patient: The door is cold.
L. G.: Excuse me? What did you say?
Patient: Cold.
L. G.: You are cold?

The patient's face reverted to its former blankness, and he did not say another word. I plan to reduce the dosage of chloral hydrate beginning tomorrow.

(signed)
Captain Lazlo C. Groth, MC USA
Chief Psychiatry Service
Pearl Harbor

r-82399
From: LAZLO C. GROTH
To: FILE
Subject: Patient MZ-54764-8
Date: 8/21/43

Forty-eight hours after reducing his chloral hydrate dosage, I am observing a marked increase in the patient's general awareness. Specifically, the patient seems to be staring at the apple on my desk. I offered to share it with him, and he became agitated, straining against the straitjacket and rolling his eyes like a trapped animal. I asked him what was wrong.

Patient: What year is this?
L. G.: It's nineteen forty-three. Why do you ask?
Patient (agitated): I'm not alive. I was—

At this point the patient paused for several seconds, as if trying to remember something, then he continued.

Patient (voice rising): I was, was, was, was, was, was, was—

He appeared to be stuck on that one word, like a person who stutters, but more so. His voice became extremely loud.

Patient (screaming): WASWASWASWASWASWAS!

At that point his eyes closed and he pitched forward out of his chair onto the floor, where he curled up into a ball, still screaming, "WASWASWAS . . ." Nothing I could do would stop him until a nurse arrived with a syringe full of sodium pentothal. I gave him an injection, and within seconds he lost consciousness and was returned to his room.

(signed)
Captain Lazlo C. Groth, MC USA
Chief Psychiatry Service
Pearl Harbor

r-82399

From: LAZLO C. GROTH

To: FILE

Subject: Patient MZ-54764-8

Date: 9/1/43

The patient has been unresponsive for four days now. We have initiated intravenous feeding and hydration.

L. G.

r-82399

From: LAZLO C. GROTH

To: FILE

Subject: Patient MZ-54764-8

Date: 7/14/45

Yesterday afternoon one of the attendants on F Ward reported that, after nearly two years in a vegetative state, the patient suddenly awakened and requested a peanut butter sandwich. When I arrived, the patient was sitting up in bed attempting to remove the bandage covering his eye. I greeted him, and suggested that he leave the bandage in place. The patient complied. (It should be noted here that the bandage covering the patient's left eye was placed there for cosmetic reasons. The eye socket was completely healed, but its appearance is such that it was upsetting to the nurses and other patients.)

Patient: I'm a little hungry.

L. G.: What would you like to eat?

Patient (staring at his hands): Peanut butter. What happened to me?

L. G.: You were injured. Don't you remember?

Patient: If I remembered I wouldn't be asking you.

L. G.: What is your name?

He opened his mouth to reply, but nothing came out. At that point the patient's face turned red and his good eye seemed to bulge, as if he were trying to force an answer from his own throat. Then he actually reached into his mouth with the fingers of his right hand and probed his tongue, as if checking to make sure it was there.

I pulled his hand from his mouth and told him to try to relax.

The patient took several deep breaths, his eye closed. He opened and closed his mouth, working his jaw back and forth.

Patient: Tell me where I am.

L. G.: You are in the Pearl Harbor Naval Hospital.

Patient: How was I hurt?

L. G.: We don't know.

Patient: What's wrong with me? I don't remember anything. I don't even know who I am.

Further attempts to question the patient elicited no response. His eyes closed and he fell into what appears to be a normal sleep.

(signed)
Captain Lazlo C. Groth, MC USA
Chief Psychiatry Service
Pearl Harbor

r-82399
From: LAZLO C. GROTH
To: FILE
Subject: Patient MZ-54764-8
Date: 7/28/45

The patient's recovery appears to be complete but for the fact that he claims not to remember who he is. Recently, he has taken to calling himself "Mr. Was." Records show that there were no U.S. military personnel by that name stationed in the Solomon Islands.

I have met with the patient daily over the past two weeks. He is friendly and talkative unless I broach the subject of his identity or his past, at which point he becomes agitated. I have not seen any need for restraints at this point, although an orderly is present during our interviews.

The patient claims to have been experiencing vivid dreams, most of them having to do with a metal door. Other objects that have appeared repeatedly in his dreams include a baseball bat, a dog, and a girl with green eyes. Very little seems to happen in his dreams. In every case, he feels as though he is propelled through a landscape by some unidentified force, with no volition of his own.

The patient is willing to discuss his dreams, but I notice that he becomes tense and pale while doing so.

At this point, I am unable to determine whether the patient's amnesia is actual or feigned. I plan to administer a moderate dosage of scopolamine before our session tomorrow afternoon.

(signed)
Captain Lazlo C. Groth, MC USA
Chief Psychiatry Service
Pearl Harbor

r-82399
From: LAZLO C. GROTH
To: COLONEL CHARLES FREEMAN
Deputy Director, Office of Strategic Services
Washington, D.C.
Date: 8/25/45

Dear Chuck,

Now that the war is pretty much over I hope it's not too late to congratulate you on your job with the OSS. The word is, you undercover guys get a lot of the credit for bringing down der Führer and his boys. It seems a long time since our days at Kansas State! Can you still drink a bottle of beer in one gulp? Next time I'm in Washington, I'll want to see it again.

I'm writing today because of a peculiar, and probably meaningless, occurrence here at MacArthur. I decided to contact you because I heard through the grapevine that the OSS is taking a particular interest in maintaining security around the new atomic weapons program. I don't know whether or not that is true, but if you aren't the right person to contact with this, perhaps you can rechannel the information. In any case, here is what happened.

We have a patient here who was found wandering around naked on Guadalcanal two years ago. As near as we can tell from his behavior and speech, he's an American, but we don't know what his name is, and neither does he. Or so he claims.

Shortly after arriving here at MacArthur, the patient lapsed into something resembling a catatonic state, and remained unresponsive for nearly two years. One month ago he spontaneously regained his ability to move about and interact with our staff. He seems perfectly normal now, except that he has adopted the nonsense name of "Mr. Was," and he insists that he has absolutely no memory of who he is. I encouraged him to keep a journal, in hopes that he would provide some clues to his origins, but it hasn't helped.

On 7/29/45, I injected the patient with scopolamine before interviewing him. We learned nothing about his identity, but the patient made some odd comments which, at the time, seemed meaningless. He told me that the Japanese would keep coming until they were stopped by "the atom bomb." I had never heard of the atom bomb before, and I assumed he was talking nonsense.

That interview took place about one week *before* we dropped the big one on Hiroshima.

Coincidence? Probably, but it's been weighing on my mind ever since, and when I heard you'd signed on as DD of the OSS, I thought I'd bring it to your attention. Until our patient uttered the words "atom bomb," neither I nor anyone I know had ever heard of such a weapon.

I am enclosing a transcript of that interview.

That's all, Chuck. I don't know whether this fellow is for real or not, but since the atomic program is of such importance, I felt the need to pass this information along.

(signed)
Captain Lazlo C. Groth, MC USA
Chief Psychiatry Service
Pearl Harbor

enclosed: transcript: interview: MZ-54764-8

Transcript of interview with patient MZ-54764-8 on 7/29/45 (15 minutes after administration of scopolamine)

Dr. Lazlo Groth: Can you hear me?

MZ-54764-8: No.

L. G.: I know you can hear me.

MZ: Okay.

L. G.: Do you know who I am?

MZ: Dr. Groth. The headshrinker.

L. G.: What is your name?

MZ: Mr. Was.

L. G.: Do you remember your mother?

MZ: (silence)

L. G.: Do you remember being on Guadalcanal? In the jungle?

MZ: Jungle.

L. G.: Yes. What happened to you?

MZ: Rain. Japanese. Thousands of Japs.

L. G.: Yes?

MZ: They keep coming. Have to stop them.

L. G.: What do you do? How do you stop them?

MZ: The bomb.

L. G.: What bomb?

MZ: The atom bomb.

L. G.: What is that?

MZ: We stop them with the atom bomb.

L. G.: What is "the atom bomb"?

MZ: (laughs)

L. G.: What is your name?

MZ: Mr. Was.

L. G.: What happened to you on Guadalcanal?

MZ: I died.

**TOP SECRET**

From: COLONEL CHARLES FREEMAN
Deputy Director, Office of Strategic Services
Washington, D.C.
To: CAPTAIN LAZLO C. GROTH MC USA
Chief Psychiatry Service
Pearl Harbor Naval Hospital
Pearl Harbor, Hawaii
Date: 9/1/45

Lazy:

I'll be there with my team before you can say "chug-a-lug." The patient is to be kept segregated from other patients and nonessential staff until our arrival. Please prepare the patient for transfer to D.C. *DO NOT* conduct any further interviews.

Chuck

P.S. You mentioned something about the patient keeping a journal. Please confiscate same pending our arrival.

*The body of the third notebook is a collection of unlined pages punched and bound into the three-ring binder. The handwriting in the early sections is small, close-spaced, and dark. The paper is frequently torn or punctured, as if the writer were pressing the pen with great force into the page.*

*—P. H.*

*(undated)*

Dr. Groth suggested that I keep this journal. He said it might help me find out who I am. He said that the things we write are often revealing, that one day a clue to my identity might flow from the tip of this ballpoint pen. Frankly, I think he's full of crap, but what else is there to do here?

The first thing I remember is waking up and no one was there. The corners of the room looked flat and dimensionless. I moved my hand toward my face, felt the bandage over my eye.

I sat up. My gut felt like a bag full of needles and knives. I saw flashes of jungle, smelled burning, heard machine-gun fire, a wall of fire.

The vision passed, I returned to the flat room with the white walls.

I had no idea where I was. Or who I was.

My hands were stiff and clumsy, but I got hold of the chart hanging at the foot of the bed.

*Patient #MZ-54764-8.*

I had no name.

Doctor Groth warned me not to expect too much. He said I would look different.

"The surgeons had to rebuild much of your face," he said. "But there's a good chance you'll recognize yourself."

He handed me a mirror, and I looked upon my face for the first time.

My stomach went cold and I began to shake.

It wasn't the scars. I had expected that. Even the collapsed left eye didn't bother me so much. What really got me, what made my guts spin, was the fact that the face in the mirror looked utterly unfamiliar. With or without the scars and bruises, I had never seen this man before.

They showed me a list of MIAs, soldiers who had disappeared on Guadalcanal, the small Pacific island where I had been found. One of these names must be yours, they told me. I looked at each of the names on the list, but not one of them was even remotely familiar. They left a copy by my bedside.

It was a game to them. They tried everything they knew to get a name out of me, but I had none to give.

Nurse Bass would come in with a tray of tasteless hospital food. "And how are we today?" she would say, smiling, chin thrust forward, dark eyebrows waggling.

"Fine," I would say.

"Isn't it a nice day?"

"Yes it is," I would reply, thinking it a stupid question because, as I had learned, we were in Hawaii, where it is always a nice day, and in any case I had no window. It could have been any sort of day at all.

"*What's your name?*" Nurse Bass would ask with sudden intensity, shoving her pointed chin in my face, attempting to startle the missing information from my scrambled brain. She got nothing from me.

One day I overheard a couple of the doctors talking about someone named "Mr. Was." After a moment, I realized that they were talking about me. At our next meeting, I asked Dr. Groth why they were calling me Mr. Was. He seemed embarrassed, but then explained that I'd had some sort of fit when I first arrived at the hospital and had screamed the word "was" repeatedly. It must have been some fit.

I was sitting up in bed reading *Stars and Stripes* later that day when Nurse Bass sneaked up behind me.

"What's your name!" she barked.

I decided I was sick of it. I told her my name was Mr. Was.

She seemed disappointed. "Was?"

"Yes. Mr. Was. W-A-S, *Was*. Mr. Was." It was better than nothing, I decided.

She frowned and said, "Do you have a first name?"

"No."

A few days later Dr. Groth came in and, for about the five hundredth time, asked me my name.

"My name is Mr. Was," I said.

He looked at a clipboard in his hand, then said, "I see."

"Your name is *See?* I never met anyone named *See* before." I was being difficult, I know, but there wasn't a lot else to do.

The doctor pursed his lips.

"You're a headshrinker, right?"

He smiled, somewhat to my surprise. "That's right," he said.

"Then you know all about the mind, right?"

"I know a little."

"So how come I don't know who I am?"

"That's what we hope to find out, son. For starters, we know your name isn't *Was.*"

That bugged me. If he didn't know who I was, how could he be telling me with such certainty who I wasn't?

"Until I say different," I said, "my name is Was."

I don't know what that stuff was that Doc Groth stuck me with, but it left me with no memory of our talk and one monster of a headache. The next day, he came in and asked me what an "atom bomb" was. I told him it was a really big bomb. He laughed and asked me why a really big bomb would be named after the smallest particle in the universe.

I don't know, I just hope he never gives me any of that stuff again.

The Japanese army surrendered to General Douglas MacArthur today, September 2, and we are celebrating with cake and Coca-Cola. The doctors and staff were drinking something else from paper cups. I took the opportunity to ask Dr. Groth when I would be released.

"Where do you want to go?" he asked.

"I don't know," I told him. "But I'm not getting anywhere sitting around here. I feel fine." I did feel fine—or at least as fine as a one-eyed, crook-armed, scarred-up amnesiac *could* feel.

Dr. Groth took a sip from his cup and rested a hand on my shoulder. "You're going to have a visitor soon," he said. "Then we'll know more."

"Who?"

"A friend of mine from Washington, Colonel Chuck Freeman. He's very interested in your case. He's flying in tomorrow."

*Copies of the following letters were inserted into the binder at this point.*

*—P. H.*

From: VINCENT C. YEDDIS
Director, U.S. Institute of Psychopharmacological Research
To: COLONEL CHARLES FREEMAN
Deputy Director, Office of Strategic Services
Washington, D.C.
Date: January 4, 1946

Dear Colonel Freeman:

Subject MZ-54764-8 remains unresponsive to our questions. I am concerned that increasing levels of T-382 may cause damage beyond that which the subject has experienced. I am compelled to say at this point that despite what the Germans have told us, the drug appears to be nothing more than a strong sedative with hallucinatory side effects, and not the "truth serum" they claim it to be. Although some subjects have been successfully interrogated under its influence, I suspect that better result could be achieved by giving them a few stiff drinks or, failing that, a rubber hose applied smartly to the soles of their feet.

Just kidding.

Please advise.

(signed)
Vincent C. Yeddis

From: VINCENT C. YEDDIS
Director, U.S. Institute of Psychopharmacological Research
To: COLONEL CHARLES FREEMAN
Deputy Director, Office of Strategic Services
Washington, D.C.
Date: January 11, 1946

Dear Colonel Freeman:

Again, my apologies for the flippant tone of my recent memo. I have been under a good deal of pressure here. Nevertheless, my doubts about the efficacy of T-382 remain.

Per our conversation of January 7, we increased the dosage of T-382 for subject MZ-54764-8 by 300 mg. As in previous trials, the subject immediately fell into a deep sleep, and was revived by the application of ice packs to his feet, abdomen, and neck. Following is a transcript of the resulting interview:

VY: Can you hear me?
MZ-54764-8: (no response)
VY: Can you hear me?
MZ-54764-8: (no response)
VY: If you can hear me, blink your eyes.
MZ-54764-8: (no response)

At that point the patient began to shake. His hands clenched and unclenched spasmodically, his eye rolled up, his face went red, and foamy saliva began running down his chin. Shortly thereafter, he became unconscious, and remained so for the next twenty-four hours.

He is now awake, or at least his eye is open and blinking from time to time, but he has slipped into what appears to be a classic catatonic state. He cannot walk, feed himself, or use the toilet.

In my opinion, any further use of T-382 to coerce information from this man might completely destroy whatever is left of his mind, and I must refuse to participate.

Please advise.

(signed)
Vincent C. Yeddis

*According to documents obtained under the Freedom of Information Act, Vincent C. Yeddis was transferred from the U.S. Institute of Psychopharmacological Research in Washington to the U.S. Naval Base at Chillum Bay, Alaska, on February 19, 1946. He was temporarily replaced by Colonel C. Capstone, an OSS officer.*

*The following May, Colonel Capstone left his position at the IPR and patient MZ-54764-8 was admitted to Salisbury Acres, a private mental hospital in Virginia. The administrator of Salisbury Acres was instructed to forward all bills to a post office box in Washington, D.C.*

*Hospital records state that the patient slowly regained his ability to feed himself, and by 1952 he was able to move about and to respond to simple commands, although he remained unable or unwilling to speak. There is no record, however, of the patient uttering a single word until January 30, 1993, when a young orderly named Nong Tran, in direct violation of hospital policy, performed an acupuncture procedure on the uncomplaining MZ-54764-8.*

*In the following section of the diary, the handwriting changes considerably. The letters are larger, and the pen is not pressed so hard against the paper. Presumably this is due to the writer's advancing age.*

*—P. H.*

February 1, 1993
New Orleans, Louisiana

I am sitting at a long table in the Café du Monde, drinking café au lait. Although it is four o'clock in the morning, there are still plenty of people on the street here in the French Quarter. It is a strange place, a city-within-a-city where one can be both surrounded by people, and alone.

In my case, I am accompanied by Patient MZ-54764-8, Mr. Was, and Corporal John R. Lund. We are all sipping from the same chunky ceramic cup. Every few minutes I turn a page in this thick notebook, wondering whether it will open up into my forgotten past.

I sip my café au lait and wonder if they are looking for me.

The young man who picked me up hitchhiking back in Virginia told me he was on his way to New Orleans for Mardi Gras. That's tomorrow. He was a nice man, and he didn't ask me too many questions. His name was Bobby Dennison. I told him that I, too, wished to celebrate Mardi Gras.

He said, "No kidding? I hope I still got *my* party legs when I'm your age, old-timer!" We drove straight through the night. He dropped me off on Bourbon Street in front of the Royal Sonesta, where he said he had a room reserved. That was a few hours ago.

Bobby was a nice man, and I feel terrible about stealing his wallet. I hope it doesn't spoil his vacation. The thing was, I had no money. Nothing. Not even a real name. I needed the money to maneuver in this strange new world. One good thing is that the wallet I stole was a fat one. Bobby had brought close to a thousand dollars to Mardi Gras. I think that's a lot of money, although I am quickly learning that here in 1993, a cup of coffee can cost you a dollar or more.

So I've been sitting here in the Café du Monde, trying to make sense of these papers.

The funny thing is, I remember everything from the time I woke up in the hospital in Hawaii. I remember the things they did to me in Washington. I remember all the questions, the injections, the ice packs. I even remember the long years filled with months filled with days when I lay in bed counting the number of holes in the white ceiling tiles, or walking about the hospital grounds like a zombie, feeling nothing but the slow, constant passing of time. I remember most clearly the Asian orderly who came to me in the night with his needles.

He introduced himself to me as Nong.

"But you can call me Freddie," he said in his quiet, singsong voice.

As always, I stared blankly back at him, unable to respond.

Freddie told me he was from Vietnam, that he had received his medical training there, and had practiced traditional medicine in Hanoi and Hong Kong before coming to the United States. He went on about this for some time, though he had no reason to believe I could hear him. Maybe he simply enjoyed the opportunity to tell his story without being interrupted.

As he spoke he examined my body, pressing here and there, with special attention to my feet, my hands, and my neck. Some of the places he touched seemed incredibly sensitive, sending tremors through my limbs. Having felt nothing for years, the effects startled me. Freddie must have seen some change in my face. He smiled, winked, and continued with his story.

It seemed that Freddie had a hard time becoming accepted by the American medical community. He would have to spend another five years in medical school here before being allowed to treat patients, and many of his proven traditional therapies were a bit strange, including something called "acupuncture," which had been his specialty in the Far East. I had never heard of acupuncture, and when he pulled out his leather and velvet case and showed me the wickedly long needles, I thought it was the end. The drugs and the ice packs had been nothing compared to this. If I could have screamed, I would have. With growing horror, I listened to him describe the theories and practice of acupuncture—

A man sweeping between the tables keeps giving me a look. I've been sitting here for two hours and bought only this one cup of coffee. I guess I'd better move on.

February 2, 1993

I have taken a room at the Blue Bayou Motor Inn, a mile and a half north of the French Quarter. The carpet stinks of cigarettes and spilled beer, the mattress is lumpy, and the television doesn't work. It cost me eighty-five dollars, but I feel lucky to have found a room at all in this crazy city. The street is filled with revelers, some kind of parade, people in costumes and masks, every one of whom knows exactly who they are.

Last night's dream was a real doozy. I dreamed I was standing in an apple orchard hitting apples with a baseball bat. The apples were filled with blood. Each apple I hit would explode in a warm red shower.

The memories are easier to take, but no less spooky. A few days ago I passed a young girl on the street. She was about fifteen, I'd guess, with red hair and a bounce in her walk. I suddenly remembered a girl in a polka-dot dress sitting across a table covered with bowls and plates piled high with food, grinning at me, her green eyes catching the light, flickering.

I wonder who she was.

I was writing earlier about Freddie. As he was showing me his needles, some of which were over six inches long, he explained to me that he was going to perform a procedure that had been used in China for thousands of years to help people who suffered from a form of paralysis called "ancestor blight." Ancestor blight, Freddie explained, struck those who were thrown into inharmonious contact with their reincarnated ancestors.

"For instance," he said, "suppose you go into a store to buy a loaf of bread, and the clerk is rude to you. You argue with the clerk, and much bad feeling fills the air. Now, if the clerk is your reincarnated great-grandfather, you might suffer from the blight. You might, for instance, forget how to tie your shoe the next day. In worse cases, you might neglect an important appointment. In the very worst cases, you might forget how to be alive."

At that point, having received no response from me, Freddie proceeded to insert his long, shiny needles deep into my blighted body.

I didn't feel a thing. He might as well have been pushing them into a straw doll. The procedure went on for some time, with no apparent effect. Some time before dawn, Freddie removed his needles and left my room. I fell asleep.

And I dreamed about the door. Even as I dreamed, I knew I had been there before. I dreamed of stepping through a short metal door, stepping out into a lush green sunlit world. A bearded man stood with a woman in a black dress and their two daughters, looking at something behind me. I turned, and saw an image of myself, my face contorted, my hands dripping blood, a baseball bat in my hands. I reached out and took the bat from myself, hurled it into the air. My image collapsed.

The next morning when the orderly brought my breakfast, I said, "Thank you."

Her jaw dropped, and she ran from my room.

I had spoken for the first time in nearly half a century.

The next day I was escorted to the office of Dr. Berringer, the hospital administrator. He sat at his desk reading a thick file. The orderly guided me to a chair, crossed his arms, and watched. Dr. Berringer continued to read the file, looking up at me occasionally.

"Well, now," he said at last, pulling his reading glasses down toward the tip of his long nose, "I understand you're with us again."

"Have I been gone?" I asked.

He smiled. "In a sense, yes. You've been here now for forty-seven years, but you haven't exactly been *with* us. I've been administrator here for over a decade, and according to your records, you haven't uttered a word until this morning."

I shrugged. I didn't trust this doctor. I vividly remembered the drugs and the ice.

"I understand that you had a visit from our Mr. Tran."

"You mean Freddie?"

"Yes. Mr. Tran."

"I'd like to see him again," I said.

Dr. Berringer's face plunged into one of those offended doctor frowns, flared nostrils and all. "Mr. Tran has been relieved of his responsibilities here at Salisbury," he said.

I stared back at him.

He cleared his throat. "What do you remember?"

"I remember Hawaii. I remember Washington."

"Do you remember your name?"

I did not. I remembered nothing of my life before waking up in the naval hospital in Hawaii. I shook my head.

"You have a tag on your file," he said. "I doubt they still have much interest in your case after all these years, but I've notified the proper authorities that you have regained your powers of speech. I hope you'll cooperate with them should they choose to ask you a few questions."

"Of course," I said.

That was when I knew I'd have to leave Salisbury Acres, and the sooner the better. That night I let myself out of my room, slipping the lock with a piece of wire from my bedsprings. For some reason, I knew how to get through doors.

I had been at Salisbury for so long, I knew the orderlies' routines. It was a simple matter to make my way undetected through the hospital up to the fourth floor, where I broke into Dr. Berringer's office, again using the bedspring wire as a key.

My file still sat on his desk, a sheaf of official-looking papers and this notebook filled with writing I recognized as my own. I also found a shirt, suit, and tie hanging in a closet in his office. My hospital slippers didn't exactly go with the tie, and the jacket was a bit large, but it was no time to be picky.

One hour later I was sitting in Bobby Dennison's Olds, heading for New Orleans.

The big question in my mind now is, What next?

I turn again to the yellowed letter I'd found tucked into the back of the notebook.

**T O P  S E C R E T**

From: COLONEL CHARLES FREEMAN
Office of Strategic Services
Washington, D.C.

To: CALVIN CAPSTONE
Director, U.S. Institute of Psychopharmacological Research

Date: May 2, 1946

Re: #MZ-54764-8:

Subject has been identified as Corporal John R. "Jack" Lund of Memory, Minnesota. He has been determined to be of no further interest to OSS. However, it is our feeling that further confinement is indicated. Please transfer subject to Salisbury effective immediately and instruct an indefinite course of sedation. Subject is not to be informed of his identity until such time as the OSS deems it advisable.

(signed)
Colonel Charles Freeman
Deputy Director

So who am I?

I do not remember being Corporal John R. "Jack" Lund.

For nearly fifty years I have thought of myself as Mr. Was, while the nurses and orderlies have thought of me as MZ-54764-8. Only a select few Washington bureaucrats—probably dead or retired by now— knew me to be this John Lund person.

I look in the warped mirror of this cheap motel room. My skin is still smooth from years spent indoors and expressionless, but the white hair, the yellow teeth, and the bristly eyebrows reveal a man in his late sixties or early seventies. That means I have been Mr. Was for much, much longer than I had been John Lund.

Nevertheless, I feel I must journey to this place called Memory.

How ironic.

February 17, 1993
Memory, Minnesota

I bought a '75 Chevy for three hundred dollars in New Orleans. The thing burned a quart of oil every hundred miles, but it got me here, to Memory.

I pulled in late last night. The only business in town that was open was a little joint called Ole's Quick Stop, a sort of convenience store with a little liquor bar at one end. Even before I stepped in through the door, I knew I'd been there before. I *remembered* the man behind the bar, a sour-faced man in his forties. I knew his name was Ole, but I didn't know how or why or when the knowledge had come to be in my mind. I felt as if I were in a dream, as though none of what I was seeing was real. At the same time, I knew it was.

At the other end of the room, a pair of aging, grossly overweight men wearing identical plaid flannel shirts were shooting pool. They paused long enough to give me the once-over. I had the feeling they didn't get many strangers in this town. I smiled and nodded. They looked at one another, then back at me, then returned to their game.

I took a seat at the bar and asked for a Coca-Cola. The bartender popped open a can of Coke and set it before me. I took a sip and wondered what I should do next. On the one hand, I thought I should dive right into it and start asking questions. On the other hand, I wanted to lay low and get a feel for the town, see what would happen.

"Slow night?" I asked.

"Just like always," growled the bartender.

"How many people live in this town?"

"Not enough," he said.

The door opened, and a man wearing a long wool coat and a gray felt fedora entered.

"Or maybe too many," the bartender added, frowning at the newcomer. "Depends on your point a view."

"A bottle of Gordon's gin, if you please," said the man in the hat, stopping a few feet short of the bar. His creaky voice had a nasty, demanding edge to it. I turned my head to look at him. He was old, like me. Deep lines framed his wide, downturned mouth. His neck sagged with wrinkled flesh.

The bartender took a bottle from the wall behind the bar and slid it into a paper bag.

"That'll be twelve fifty."

"Put it on my account," the man snapped. He stepped up to the bar then, took the bottle, then turned his face directly toward me. A livid scar running along his jaw jumped out at me, and suddenly it hit me. I couldn't recall his name, but I *knew* him. I not only knew him but, for some reason, I was afraid of him.

He locked his eyes on my face. I could feel my heart beating in my throat.

He said, "You in the war? That how you got all banged up? Your face?" He pointed at his scarred jaw. "Me, I got this."

I forced myself to nod. My heartbeat slowed. I said, "I don't remember what happened to me."

He nodded and rubbed his forefinger along his jaw. "Which ocean you cross?"

"I think the Pacific."

"Me, too. What's your name?"

I hesitated, then decided to go for it. "Lund," I said. "John Lund."

The effect on the old man would have been funny if it wasn't so all-out eerie. For two or three seconds his expression froze as if someone had stopped time.

"No, you aren't," he said. His eyes darted back and forth across my features. "You can't be." He blinked and took a step back. He must have seen something in my face then, something that made him believe me. His mouth fell open and he went dead white except for a purple swelling around his eyes, which bulged out of his head so far, I thought they might explode.

"You're dead," he croaked. He stood up, staggered back a few steps, then dropped to his knees clutching his chest and making a whistling noise in his throat. I stayed on my stool, too astonished to move.

The bartender shouted, "Mr. Skoro! Mr. Skoro? You okay there?"

As the old man fell face-first to the grimy floor, I thought, so that's his name. *Skoro.*

I knew that name, but I hadn't a clue what it had to do with me.

The bartender rushed around the end of the bar and turned him over. He shouted at one of the pool players, who were staring slack-jawed at the man on the floor. "Hermie, get your van around front here. We gotta get him to a doctor. Hurry up! He could be dying."

Hermie—I remembered his name, too—set his pool cue on the table.

"I s'pose I could do that," he said. "Only I got to tell you, Ole, I ain't gonna be too terrible sad if he don't make it." He turned toward the other pool player. "How 'bout you, Harry?"

Harry shrugged.

I remembered Harry now, too.

Ole said, "Doggone it, you boys let him die on my floor,

you'll be driving all the way to Red Wing every time you want a drink. You understand me?"

Once Hermie and Harry got moving, they had Skoro into the back of the van within two minutes. Ole and I stood in front of the Quick Stop and watched their taillights disappear up the road.

Ole shook his head. "Those boys ain't got the sense of a dead dog between 'em," he muttered. "How they got to be that old being that stupid, I'll never know."

"You think he'll be all right?" I asked.

"Skoro? Couldn't say. He's a tough old bird."

"He lives in town here?"

Ole gestured with a thumb. "Up atop the bluff. Big old place. Boggs's End, we call it."

I looked up the bluff and saw the shape of a big house backlit by a half-moon. A closeup of its weathered gray clapboard siding swam into my mind's eye. I was sure I had been there before.

"Does he live alone?" I asked.

"You kidding? Who else would want to live in a spookhole like that?"

"I was wondering if we should notify someone."

"Well . . . he's got a daughter, lives down in Illinois. I don't imagine there's much she could do from down there, but I'm sure folks at the hospital will call her."

"So how long has Skoro lived around here?"

"He ain't never lived anyplace else, far as I know."

Although I could see Boggs's End from Ole's, it was still a long way off, and the roads in this part of the country are twisted up like a pail of worms. I was prepared to get lost, but it seemed like as soon as I started the car, I just knew which way to go. Ten minutes later I was parked in front of the wide, sagging veranda. The feeling that I was walking backward through my life overwhelmed me. I remembered everything I saw, but nothing else.

I didn't bother to knock. The doors were unlocked. I stepped into Boggs's End, each step echoed in my mind.

The foyer with the cold marble floor. The cracked leather sofa. The smell of old wood. The chandelier.

My hunger to recover my early years grew with each shred of recaptured past. I had been there before, many times. My hands were shaking. I stood beneath the chandelier and closed my eyes and listened to my pulse throbbing in my ears. Was I excited, or afraid?

I must see it all, I told myself. I must remember everything.

Then I heard a soft, repeated clicking sound. I turned my head from side to side, trying to locate the noise. It was coming from the back of the house. I moved toward it, past the white marble staircase, down the short hallway, into the library that looked out over the bluff.

I remembered the room, and the books.

But I did not remember the big man in overalls sitting at the desk working at the computer.

Too surprised to move, I stood in the doorway and watched his thick fingers rattling the keyboard. He was a large man, broad across the back, with black curly hair tumbling from beneath a wide-brimmed black hat. A matching beard sprouted from his weathered face and spilled over his chest. As I watched, he peered intently at the numbers on the computer screen, frowned, and muttered to himself. "Primitive, it was. I will be glad when it hasn't been invented yet, I was!" He typed furiously for several seconds. Rows and columns of digits flickered. "Will be too many parts. Those blasted doors. Too complicated. Too complicated." He continued to type, muttering all the while.

I cleared my throat.

He turned his big bearded face toward me and fixed me with a pair of eyes so dark they looked like holes. "Good day, sir," he said, grinning. He had one of those voices that you can feel in your chest. "You don't remember me, I see. It had been a long time."

"Been a long time since what?" I asked.

"Know you what tomorrow is?"

I shook my head.

The man laughed. "Tomorrow was the day you became."

"I don't understand."

"You'll have to write it down," he said, "to read it."

"Write what down? Who are you?"

"I was nobody yet. But you can call me Pinky." He returned his attention to the computer.

Even if I knew what was going on here, I thought, it wouldn't make sense.

"This man Skoro, he cheats." Pinky pointed at a square of wrinkled, yellowed paper taped to the wall beside the desk. "Have you seen?"

I stepped closer and looked. It was a piece of newspaper covered with tiny print. Some kind of statistics. Stock tables.

"You will have looked at the date," Pinky said.

I looked. The paper was dated 1996. Three years in the future.

"A misprint?" I asked.

"A cheat sheet," he said. "An anachronism. Out of place, out of time. A very bad thing, very bad indeed. He makes much money using this paper. Stocks and bonds are not for knowing, they are for guessing. But he knows for years and years which companies will still exist, which little investments will grow. You call it something in this time. You call it insider trading. This is what I am saying. Your grandfather cannot do this thing. He cannot steal time yet to come."

"My grandfather," I said. "Skoro is my grandfather. I remember now."

"You will remember more, though you may think it too late. Still, you will have what life I could allow you. Your role must have been played out." He hit several keys, and the numbers on the computer screen jumped. "Neither he nor his offspring may profit," he said under his breath.

I was getting irritated by Pinky's weird way of talking.

"What are you doing here?" I said.

"This is where the disruption began," he said. "My fault, my fault, a door without locks is a fool's door. A good thing your grandfather feared what he does not know. He fears the door so much he was never able to pass through, though he tried. His body stops itself from taking the necessary step. Had he passed, I might never have been able to bring the passageways back into balance. He was a coward, afraid of both the was and the will be. This was why he changed his name. He could not abide his past. He thought he could not stand to be his father's son. But it was himself he could not stand to be. Like you, Jack Lund."

I said, "My grandfather?"

"You are confused. It will have come to you later or sooner, once you have met your echo."

He touched a key. All the numbers on the screen flickered and became nines.

I said, "What are you doing?"

"I am going to have be draining it, I did, primitive thing, it spills knowledge like an overfilled dam." The nines became eights, then sevens. "Neither he nor his offspring." Sixes. "What goes around comes around, my friend." His arm shot out and his chunky right hand slapped against the 1996 stock tables. The numbers on the computer screen continued to count down.

Fours, threes. He made a fist and the yellowed newspaper disappeared into his meaty hand.

Twos.

Ones.

Zeroes.

The screen flashed and flickered with green snow.

Pinky laughed. "All gone. Perhaps you had remembered something of me now. It mattered not."

In that instant, I saw him standing in a field of grass, a woman and two children at his side, thunderclouds filling the sky beyond.

I squeezed my eyes closed, opened them, saw his wide back disappearing out the doorway.

I heard the front door slam.

The computer screen had gone dark but for a single line of type: WHAT GOES AROUND COMES AROUND.

I looked at those words for a long time. Maybe half an hour, maybe not so long, trying to absorb all I'd heard. Not for the first time, I wondered whether I was insane. Perhaps Salisbury Acres was a mental hospital where I had been confined to treat my delusions.

Was I a madman, living in a reality that existed only in my mind?

It was possible, and certainly easier to swallow than the notion that my grandfather and I were the same age. Or that, as the bearded man had implied, time had somehow become twisted and warped. But I didn't believe that I was mad. A madman would have believed everything Pinky had said. I believed little of it.

If anyone was insane, it was Pinky.

I found a switch on the back of the computer and turned it off. The faint humming of the hard drive ceased, and the silence of the big house pressed in on me. I decided to get up, move around, see what other memories Boggs's End might unleash.

I walked down the hall to the staircase. I had a feeling that the upper floors contained my most important memories, but I was afraid.

Don't be ridiculous, I said to myself. That crazy Pinky has you spooked. I started up the staircase. After a few steps, I felt as if the soles of my shoes were not gripping the stairs, as if they had been oiled. I grabbed the banister for support and looked down.

I was standing in a puddle of blood.

I looked back. Behind me it flowed like a river of thick wine down the marble stairs. I looked up toward the landing. More blood, a red cascade running over my shoes. Slowly, I backed down the stairs, my shoes making a sucking sound each time I lifted my feet. I had to get out. Reaching the bottom, I turned toward the front entrance. The doors were not as they had been. They were shattered, one of them torn off its hinges. Black tire tracks scarred the white marble floor, and someone was screaming. Clapping my hands over my ears, I ran out through the shattered doorway, but the screaming only got louder. On some level I knew that I was the one who was screaming, but I couldn't make myself stop until all the air from inside that house had left my lungs. I tore open the car door, tumbled inside, and locked the doors.

Boggs's End stood dark and silent before me, the front doors closed and undamaged.

Now who's the crazy man, I wondered.

Memory, Minnesota
February 20, 1993

I have not been able to force myself to return to Boggs's End. The very thought of it makes my heart shake. But I did attend Skoro's funeral. I was not disappointed to find that it was to be a closed-casket service. I had no desire to look upon his face again. Apparently, he'd had few friends at the end of his life. There were fewer than a dozen people at the service, mostly people my age or older, people who would be sharing Skoro's experience soon. One younger couple, a man and woman in their early forties, occupied the front pew. Both of them looked intensely familiar, and I was sure I remembered their faces from my childhood. Or, since that would have been impossible, the faces of some people who looked like them.

I am certain they are related to me, and I fear they are insane.

They seem to think they have an invisible child.

First, I noticed they were sitting a good three feet apart from one another, which is odd for a married couple in public. When the woman spoke to her husband she would lean forward, as if trying to peer around someone. At times she would say something to the invisible person between them, or she would rest her hand on its invisible shoulder. The man had a haggard, hungover look. As I looked at him, I became unaccountably angry. When he tousled the head of the invisible child, I found myself wanting to reach over and strike him. For some reason, the words of the bearded man kept running through my head. *What goes around comes around.* At one point during the service, I realized with a jolt that I had been whispering the words aloud, over and over, like a mantra. I'm surprised I wasn't asked to leave.

The burial took place at a small nondenominational cemetery just outside of Memory. I watched from my car, confused, depressed, and feeling as if I knew even less than I had before. After the casket was lowered, as the mourners filed back to their automobiles, I got out and approached the woman, my presumed relative, with the intention of introducing myself and offering my condolences. I was only a few feet away from her when her face exploded. Blood covered her face, streaked her hair, soaked the lapels of her black wool coat. My knees went weak, and I staggered backward. She continued toward her car with her husband, whose hands were dripping blood, and their invisible child. I grabbed a tombstone for support and closed my eyes. When I opened them, they were climbing into their car, not a speck of blood on them.

## THE FOURTH NOTEBOOK:

# MEMORY

*This cardboard-covered, spiral notebook appears to be a continuation of the first notebook, written in the same shaky hand.*

*—P. H.*

Andrea Island, Puerto Rico
August 27, 1952

Andie has asked me to finish my story. She says a story isn't really a story until it is completely told. "But I filled up the notebook you gave to me!" I said. She gave me this new one. Ah, well. What else do I have to do?

After Skoro's funeral, I became convinced that I was insane, but I never once considered returning to the hospital. If a half century of confinement at Salisbury Acres had not restored my sanity, why should I consider going back? Instead, having nowhere else to go, I rented an old house trailer set back in the woods, a few miles outside of Memory. If I was a madman, I might as well be a free madman.

In the mornings I would walk the countryside, searching within my own mind for the key to my past. Often, my walks would take me near Boggs's End. I could not shake the feeling that my past lay within its walls but, even though it stood vacant, my fear would not allow me to enter that house of bloody visions.

So I contented myself with absorbing the smaller, more easily digested memories that other parts of Memory had to offer. Memories of walking in the woods, of the pretty red-haired, green-eyed girl, of driving fast on narrow dirt roads.

Back then I believed that my lost memory existed as a whole and complete entity inside my skull. I believed that the right thought, the right reminder would cause the unraveled cloth to weave itself into a completed tapestry.

But that is not the way it happens.

Memories come back one at a time. I had a growing basket

of multicolored threads, but no pattern. Places, people, and events from my early years floated about in my head, each one separate and distinct. Weaving it all together would be a tedious, prolonged process. I did not know what came first, or how much was missing, and I had only the faintest shadow of an idea of the shape of my past.

Although I bought nothing for myself but firewood and food, the money I had stolen from Bobby Dennison quickly ran out, and I was forced to support myself by doing odd jobs for the people living in and around Memory.

As the days and weeks passed, bits and pieces of my lost childhood appeared in my thoughts. One day I remembered my mother cooking dinner in a small kitchen with striped yellow wallpaper. I had seen her face before, at Skoro's funeral.

Those days passed quickly. I was prepared to live out the rest of my life as the hermit of Memory, and I might have had I not met my mother, face-to-face, in the summer of 1995.

There is a type of mushroom called a "chanterelle" that grows under old oaks. A gourmet restaurant across the lake would buy them from me for eight dollars a pound, and during mushroom season I spent as much time as possible scouring the coulees for the yellow fungus. On the day I met my mother I had been wandering the woods for some hours, finding only a few wormy chanterelles, but enjoying myself in a quiet sort of way. I reached the edge of a neglected apple orchard and realized with a start that I was only a few dozen yards from Boggs's End. The familiar fear came over me and I turned to go back the way I'd come, when a woman's voice called out to me. "Excuse me! Are you lost?"

I shook my head, staring at her.

"Are you all right?" she asked, coming closer. She had a laundry basket in her hands. Behind her, a rope strung between two apple trees carried an assortment of shirts, pants, and underwear.

"No," I replied. "I guess I got turned around. I didn't mean to intrude."

"That's okay," she said, looking at the bag in my hand. "What are you doing?"

"I was hunting mushrooms," I said.

"My name is Betty Lund," she said. "We just moved here last month." She moved closer. "What kind of mushrooms are those? May I see?"

I showed her one of the chanterelles, which look like small yellow funnels.

"I've never seen a mushroom like that before. What's your name?"

I hesitated, then told her my name was Mr. Was.

"Do I know you?" she asked.

"I have to be going," I said.

"You look familiar."

I tried to reply, but at that instant a memory came into my mind so sharp and clear and real that the air turned solid in my lungs. I saw her on a linoleum floor, hugging her knees like a fetus, red blood soaking her green dress. I backed away, then turned, walking quickly, then ran.

"You're welcome to hunt your mushrooms here," she called after me.

Now I know I am insane, I thought.

I remembered my mother now. I remembered her flowered cotton blouses, her slim hands, her tentative voice, and her sad face. And I remembered the small V-shaped scar high on her right cheek. And I remembered that it had been caused by a blow from a man's fist.

The woman in the orchard was my mother.

But that was impossible.

Therefore I was insane.

I walked drunkenly through the woods, too preoccupied with my thoughts to avoid the fallen trees, the rocks, the face-slapping branches. I fell several times, losing my bag of mushrooms, twisting my ankle, scraping my palms. It was nearly dark when I trudged up to my rented trailer and let myself in and fell into bed.

After that, I tried to stay as far away from Boggs's End as possible. I just wanted to go quietly mad, bothering no one. For several weeks, that was exactly what I did. I lay on my bed and tried not to think, leaving the trailer only when I needed supplies, which was about once a week. Making a supply run was no small chore. My car had died two winters before, so I had to walk the three miles up River Street to Ole's Quick Stop.

On one such trip I noticed the door to the old train depot—now the Memory Institute—standing wide open. During my three years in Memory I had never known the Institute to be open at all. I'd looked through the grimy window once. It had looked to me like somebody's attic. A bunch of dusty junk. Ole told me that the guy who owned the building stopped by every now and then, but that the Institute hadn't been open any regular hours since the seventies.

One thing about going quietly and privately insane: It gets pretty boring after a while. Instead of going into Ole's, I crossed the street and peered in through the open door.

The interior of the one-room building was even more cluttered and filthy than I'd imagined. A single bare lightbulb hung head high from a cord in the center of the room. Stacks of old books, photographs, and maps were piled haphazardly on rickety-looking chairs, tables, and unidentifiable articles of furniture. The walls were covered with yellowing black-and-white photos, nearly all of which seemed to be of stern, bearded men and frowning women, all wearing too much clothing.

At the back of the room, a man was bent over a large cardboard box. He removed an old leather-bound book, snorted, tossed it across the room onto a pile of similar books.

"Another Swedish bible," he muttered. "Like I need another."

As soon as I heard his voice I recognized Pinky, the man I'd met at Boggs's End. I waited for him to notice me.

He tossed aside a few more books, then turned to me and said, "Where have you been?"

"What do you mean?" I replied.

"You can't see him, can you?"

"See who?"

"Jack Lund. Jack Lund. Jack Lund."

I shook my head, confused. "I thought I was Jack Lund."

"You are. You were. You will be."

"Who are you?"

"Who are you? You are my accident, Jack Lund. You can't see him, can you? Of course you can't. He is your echo, not now."

The man was not making any sense. I decided to change the subject, if there was one. "You told me that Skoro was my grandfather."

Pinky stood up and brushed dust from his black wool trousers. "I did?"

"Yes, when we talked up at the house. That's not possible, you know."

He shook his head. "I wasn't going to do that until before. What else did I tell you?"

"What goes around comes around."

Pinky laughed and slapped his hands against the lapels of his heavy black coat, sending out twin puffs of dust. "That was true," he said. "Do you have any more questions?"

"I met a woman in the orchard. Who was she?"

"She will be your mother."

"That's impossible, too," I said.

He shrugged. "You have lost your memory, yet you believe you know what will be and what was not possible. You are assuming that different realities cannot coexist. You assumed that it is impossible to have traveled from this time to that time, that there cannot be two of you, that your reality will be more profound than that of your echo." He paused, combing his beard with his thick fingers.

"What are you saying? Are you are saying that I traveled through time?"

"Not through. Against. Now you are going with. We are travelers together, for this moment, racing into the future. Do you understand?"

"Tell me one thing. What year was I born?"

"By your calendar? Nineteen seventy-nine."

"That's im——"

Pinky held up a hand, silencing me.

"You will remember more, but you will not like it. Do not be in such a hurry."

"Remember what?"

"Your self."

"You are not living in the present. But then, who was?" He looked at his hairy wrist. There was no watch, but he said, "Look at the time! Can I help you? We're closing up here. Would you like to have bought a Swedish bible?"

"I don't think so," I said, backing out the door.

"You have things to do. Don't let me keep you. Have you spoken with your father yet? He was waiting, you know. Take care now. Good day!"

The door closed. Pinky's big bearded face stared at me through the dust-coated window. I started back up the road, my mind whirling with confused images. The man was obviously mad, yet all that he had said—senseless as it was—rang true.

I headed back across the street toward Ole's, and had only taken a few steps when I heard a crunch of tires on gravel and looked up to see a bicycle coming at me, moving fast, pedals churning, but without a rider. During the endless two seconds while I watched it coming at me, I remember thinking that I should step out of the way, but I couldn't move. I stood there stupidly until the handlebars hit me belt-high, knocking me to the ground.

The next few moments exist as a blur in my memory. I recall sitting up, wondering whether I had broken anything. As I watched, the bicycle righted itself and moved slowly away, as if someone was pushing it.

I stood up, a little shaky but nothing broken. My mind churned with a new memory.

*I was sixteen years old again, coming out of Ole's, upset because—*

A wave of dizziness rolled over me. I staggered to the side of the road and sat down.

*—because Dad was drinking again. The last thing I remembered was getting on my bike and riding—*

—that must have been when I ran into myself.

My recovered memory ended with that moment. I looked back at the Memory Institute. The light had been turned off, the CLOSED sign was propped in the window.

One thing Pinky had said reverberated in my thoughts.

*"You will remember more,"* he'd said, *"but you will not like it."*

I walked back to my rented trailer in a daze. By the time I arrived, the sun had disappeared behind the bluffs and I had rediscovered much of my past.

*I remembered growing up in Skokie.*

*I remembered friends from school.*

*I remembered the neighborhood, and the cocker spaniel named Muffer who had lived next door.*

Moving like a robot, I opened a can of sugary Boston baked beans and poured its contents into a dented aluminum saucepan. I heated it on the propane stove, spooned the beans onto slices of rye bread, and ate slowly as memories played out like a movie in my mind.

*I remembered my parents. I remembered them fighting. I remembered the time my dad had beat up my mom and then hit me in the stomach.*

*I remembered my grandfather, who had tried to kill me on his deathbed.*

*I remembered my first visit to Boggs's End.*

*I remembered the door.*

And that was when it began to make sense to me. If it was possible to travel through time, as Pinky had been trying to tell me, then it was possible that I was not insane.

*I remembered Scud.*

*I remembered Andie. I remembered visiting her with Scud, and I remembered her kissing Scud.*

That memory had lost none of its sting. It might as well have been yesterday.

I sat in a trance at that tiny table exploring my mind. I let some memories roll out slowly, relishing each moment. Other memories I had to rush through, or push aside for later. Long into the night, I played with the contents of my mind, but I could not remember my final trip into the past.

*I could not remember anything that the young Jack had not yet experienced.*

Sometime in the last dark hours, I returned in my mind to the scene that morning, to my collision with the invisible bicyclist who I now knew to be myself. Hours ago, I had remembered only events leading up to the collision. I had been unable to recall what I—the young Jack Lund—had done afterward.

*But now I remembered walking my broken bike back up the bluff. I remembered my mother in the kitchen, sitting with the table set, the food cold, waiting for me and my father to return. I remembered her locking the door. I remembered the shouting, and the sound of his car being driven through the front doors into the foyer—*

—and something released its grip on my past to clamp my heart in its icy grip—

—and *I remembered that night.*

I remembered *this* night.

Between my trailer and Boggs's End lay perhaps four miles of wooded coulee and ridge. I do not know how long it took me to make the trip—it seemed an eternity of whipping branches, stabbing thorns, and ankle-grabbing roots. I must have fallen dozens of times. By the time I burst out of the woods into the orchard, the sun had risen, my clothing was torn, and my face and hands were bloody with scratches.

The man wearing my father's face stood amongst the fallen apples. At his ankles, a few sluggish hornets buzzed over the rotting fruit. Steam rose where the low sun struck dew-coated grass. My father turned toward me, his face slack and pale, the pupils of his eyes reduced to the size of pinheads. A streak of drying blood ran up the inside of his forearm.

He said, "It's too late. She made me do it."

I shook my head. "No she didn't."

He said, "I suppose you're right." He took a few steps to the side, reached up, and tugged at the rope clothesline. "I put this up for her, you know. The dryer was broke, so I put up the clothesline for her. I did a lot of things for her. I used to have a job." He followed the rope to the branch and began working at the knot.

As I watched him, new memories solidified in my mind. I remembered lying on the floor beside my mother's body. I remember standing up and looking out the window and seeing this scene from above. I looked toward the house. There was the window, but of course I was not visible to myself.

My father had the rope untied from one tree. He dragged the loose end back along the rope's length and went to work untying the other end.

I suddenly remembered why I had made that final trip into the past. A journey of over half a century, and I had failed. I had gone back to save my mother from this man, and all for nothing. I had forgotten my mission until it was too late.

Now he was climbing the tree. He stood on one branch and tied one end of the rope to a branch higher up. He made a loop in the rope, tied another knot.

I started to walk away. I had an idea what was about to happen.

Just before I entered the woods, I heard a dull, snapping sound. I looked back. His legs were still kicking, only inches above the rotting apples.

• • •

If I was an old man then, I am a very, very old man now. It still hurts to write these words, but the pain and terror has dulled with the passing years, and I have come to accept my fate as inevitable. As Pinky would say, *It will be bound to have happened.*

I spent the next few months in my trailer, going out only to buy food, living on beans and cheap peanut butter, down to my last few dollars and with no will to go out and earn more. I might have simply stayed there and eventually starved to death, but as Pinky would say, I wasn't going to have died then.

I was on my bed buried in layers of blankets, searching my mind for a peaceful place, when someone banged on the door. They had to knock hard and repeatedly before I realized that it was a real sound, not something reverberating from my past. I rolled out of the tangle of bedding and opened the door.

It was Pinky. Behind him, a long black limousine sat idling by the roadside.

He said, "How were you?"

I shook my head.

"There is something I should not have told you." His dark eyes glittered, filled with moisture. "There is that which is permitted, and that which was forbidden. The rules will be nowhere written down. They are discovered by accident, and often never understood by those who unwittingly break them."

I must have looked confused.

Pinky said, "It is a difficult concept. I can tell you this: Those who violate the rules must pay. Some pay now, some pay later." He smiled. "Later is better."

He handed me an envelope. Writing on the front of the envelope said simply, *Jack.*

"What is this?" I asked.

"From the papers bequeathed to the Institute," he said. "You should have it."

"What's in it?"

"I don't know yet," he said. "But I did." With that, he walked back to his limo and climbed in the back. I caught a glimpse of a woman and two children inside. The limo pulled away.

I sat on the step and opened the envelope.

July 15, 1981

Dear Jack,

I know you'll never read this. But you must have known that I would never read your letters to me—and yet I did, thanks to Tadashi and Sawako Tsurumi, who came all the way from Tokyo to shatter what little peace I had left in my life.

If I have learned anything today, it is that everything I believed until now is untrue. My husband is not the man I thought I married, my daughter is doomed, and my only grandchild will not survive his eighteenth birthday. There is no happiness left for me, so I'm going to leave, as you did, as have all my loved ones, even if they do not yet know it.

Of all the terrible things you described in your letters to me, the most terrible of all was the revelation that your grandfather—your murderous grandfather—was named Skoro.

Not a common name.

It was Scud's mother's maiden name, and as soon as the war ended and Scud returned here to Memory, that's what he had his name changed to. Ever since we were kids, Scud has talked about changing his name. You remember how much he hated his father? He didn't want to be named after him. We all thought it was a bit strange—small-town folks usually stick with their birth names—but you know Scud. He made his mind up and just went and did it.

That's how I became Andrea Skoro.

It never would've happened if you'd come back alive, Jack. I can't tell you how broke up I was when I heard you were missing and probably dead. But Scud came back and we took up just like we had been before I met you, before the war. The next thing I knew, we were married. And Scud started making lots of money in the stock market, and he bought this house and had it all fixed up, and I had a baby and planted hollyhocks, and Scud planted the apple orchard, and life went on.

It was never a good marriage. Scud is a cruel man in many ways. But it was my lot to be with him, I thought.

No more. I'm getting old. He's had too much of me already. I'm going back.

The door is there, just like you said.

Scud will be back soon, looking for his dinner.

He can look for it the rest of his life.

Love,
Andie

Andrea Island, Puerto Rico
September 2, 1952

I keep thinking my story is over, but Andie wants me to keep on writing.

After reading the letter she had written to me, I knew I had to see her again.

I had to break a window to get in. Everything was gone. The furniture, the books, the pictures on the walls, all gone. I didn't care about that. I climbed the stairs, fighting off memories. I went into the third-floor closet, through the door, down the steps. The metal door was waiting for me. Without hesitating, I opened it into a moonlit night. The apple trees were bare, the grass dry and dead, but the air felt warm and moist.

She stood outside the house in a light coat, her red hair gray now, her bright green eyes dancing in nests of wrinkled flesh.

She said, "Hello, Jack."

"Andie?"

"Pinky told me I might find you here."

"Pinky? You know Pinky?"

"Yes. I thought you were dead, until he told me to come for you."

"I thought I was dead, too," I said.

She reached out a hand, and I took it.

"What time is this?" I asked.

"You don't remember this night? It's December sixth."

"It's warm," I said, remembering.

"Let's go," Andie said, tugging at my arm. We walked around the house to the driveway and got into her car, a long black Cadillac sedan. "I have a lot of money now," she said. "It's easy when you know who will win the World Series every year."

I remembered something Pinky had told me. "That's a violation of the rules," I said.

"What rules?"

"I guess it doesn't matter."

She slid behind the wheel and put the big car in gear. We rolled out of the driveway onto the dirt road.

"Where are we going?"

"We're going home. I live in the Caribbean now. No more winters."

"And what then?"

She shrugged. "And then we live for a while. At least twelve more years. I want to see my daughter one more time."

"And then?"

"Eventually we die."

I nodded. It made sense. I sank back into the leather seat and watched the trees flashing in the headlights. After a couple miles, she stopped.

"Why are we stopping?"

"Watch." She turned off the engine and the headlights. The moonlight was so bright, we could see shadows. A few minutes later, a figure emerged from the darkness, walking down the opposite side of the road. A girl with long hair. Even from a distance I knew who she was by the way she walked. The young Andie. She seemed to be holding something in her right hand, but there was nothing visible there. Nevertheless, I knew she had someone's hand. I could still feel the pressure of her fingers.

"I can see you," said my grandmother.

"I can see you," I said.

As I watched, the girl stopped. She turned toward our car, pointed. Andie let the clutch out and the car moved along the shoulder, passing the girl and her invisible companion. I looked back. She was staring at us, her eyes wide, a hand pressed to her slim white throat.

*In 1942, Andrea Skoro and Jack Lund bought a small island off the coast of Puerto Rico, where they resided for the next ten years. On September 5, 1952, though both Andrea and Jack appeared to be nearly eighty years old, the pair decided to journey to Skokie, Illinois.*

*The two traveled in their yacht, the* AndyJack, *from their island toward Miami, where they had reservations on an airliner bound for Chicago. The yacht launched in perfect weather. The sky was impossibly blue and beautiful, the waters glittered in the Caribbean sun. Their last decade had been peaceful and good and so, they believed, their lives had been worth the living. This trip was a lark, in a sense. Andrea Lund had remarked to neighbors that she was going to visit her daughter, who was about to give birth.*

*Somewhere in the Bermuda Triangle, the* AndyJack *may have encountered a bank of low clouds that the weather service had not predicted. Their radio may have failed to operate. Their compass may have spun crazily. If they emerged from the strange cloud, there may have been nothing to see. No earth, no clouds. Nothing but the sky and endless ocean.*

*The* AndyJack *was never heard from, never recovered, and never explained. Her two passengers are presumed dead.*

*Elizabeth Skoro was born in Red Wing, Minnesota, at 5:09* A.M. *on September 29, 1952, weighing seven pounds, nine and one half ounces.*

*On February 1, 1994, Mr. Robert (Bobby) Dennison approached the registration desk at the Royal Sonesta Hotel in New Orleans and discovered that his wallet was missing from his jacket pocket. Seconds later, he was approached by a man who identified himself as an attorney with Givens, Holst, and Wellcott. The attorney handed Dennison an envelope contain-*

*ing five thousand dollars in crisp, 1942 series one-hundred-dollar bills. The attorney then left without answering any of Dennison's questions, having completed the task assigned to his firm more than fifty years before.*

*Bobby Dennison went on to have the time of his life. Over the next two weeks, he spent every last dime, returning home to Virginia broke but elated. None of his friends believed his story, though he told it at every opportunity.*

*In August of 1998, an abandoned property was put up for sale by the Goodhue County in southeastern Minnesota. Jimbo Bobick, a local real estate agent, was asked to find a buyer. Because of the property's unhappy reputation, he despaired of selling it to any of the locals, and so he advertised only in Minneapolis, Chicago, and Madison newspapers. Much to his delight, he got a nibble the first week.*

*The man who called said he had been searching for just such a country retreat where he and his wife could raise their children in a safe and healthy rural environment. Jimbo assured the caller that this was the perfect property, and that the price might be negotiable.*

*The buyer showed up the next morning. He was a tall man with a strangely trimmed black beard, an odd cut of clothing, and a strange way of talking that was not quite like anything Jimbo Bobick had ever heard before.*

*He introduced himself as Mr. Boggs.*

*Through a computer search of real estate records, I finally located Mr. Pincus Q. Boggs in December 1999 in a southeastern Minnesota town called Sand, which I now believe to be the town referred to as "Memory" in the notebooks. I do not know why Jack chose to conceal the true name of the town. It may be because when he wrote his story, many of the events described had not yet occurred. I was hoping that Mr. Boggs could explain it to me.*

*Mr. Boggs agreed to meet with me at his home in Sand. I made plane reservations and flew to Minneapolis the following morning. I called Mr. Boggs from the airport to confirm our appointment, then drove the seventy-odd miles south to Sand, on the western shore of Lake Pepin.*

*It was easy to find Boggs's End. All I had to do was follow the smoke.*

*I watched as the last few timbers crumbled into ash.*

*The cause of the blaze remains, officially, a mystery.*

Pete Hautman
Charlotte, NC
December 31, 1999

Here's a sneak peek of
Pete Hautman's next book

# BLANK CONFESSION

***Available now***

Shayne Blank walks into the police station and confesses to having killed someone.

How could the quiet, unassuming new kid in town be a murderer? It's hard to believe, but as Shayne tells his story, Detective Rawls is forced to face the reality that Shayne may be more—a lot more—than he seems.

But who is he?

Five lousy minutes.

Detective George Rawls hung up the phone, brought his feet down from his cluttered desktop, looked at his watch, and sighed. If the kid had walked into the station five minutes later, Rawls's shift would have been over. He would have been driving home to enjoy a peaceful dinner with his wife.

Five more minutes and Benson would have caught this case. Rawls stood up and looked over the divider toward Rick Benson's desk. Benson, looking back at him, smirked. Rawls rolled his eyes and hitched up his pants. They kept falling down—his wife's fault, all those vegetables she'd been feeding him since his cholesterol numbers came in high.

He opened the upper left-hand drawer of his desk and took out his service revolver. Rawls was old school; he still used the weapon that had been issued to him as a rookie. He emptied the cylinder into the drawer and slid the unloaded weapon into his shoulder holster.

The unloaded gun was a prop. These young punks were impressed by such things. Most of them. He left his jacket hanging on the back of his chair and made his way out of the room and down the hallway toward the front entrance. He walked past the long citizens' bench, automatically checking out the four people sitting there: A slight, pale-faced boy—black jeans, black T-shirt, scuffed-up black cowboy boots—sat with his elbows resting on his knees, staring at the floor. Probably some middle-school bad boy picked up for shoplifting. Next was a young woman wearing a tight skirt, smeared mascara, and a nasty bruise on her right cheek. A hooker, no doubt. Then an anxious-looking older woman, probably there to report a runaway husband, or a purse snatching. At the end was a scowling middle-aged man in a rumpled suit—could be anything.

Rawls made these assessments automatically and effortlessly. Part of the job.

Directly facing the front doors of the police station, John Kramoski sat behind his elevated desk flipping through the duty roster. Rawls stopped in front of him. The desk sergeant looked up.

"Sorry, George," Kramoski said. "I know your shift is almost over, but you were up. And it's a kid—your specialty."

Rawls was the precinct's unofficial "Youth Crimes" officer. He had once believed that, working with kids, he might actually make a difference. These days he wasn't so sure.

"Where is he?" he asked.

Kramoski jerked his thumb toward the bench.

Rawls looked over, surprised. "How come he's not in the interview room?"

"He walked in here by himself. Besides, look at him. What's he gonna do?"

"We're talking about the kid on the end, right?"

"Yep."

Rawls shook his head. "He looks, like, twelve."

"Says he's sixteen."

"Jesus."

"And Mary and Joseph, bro." Kramoski returned his attention to the duty roster.

Rawls walked back down the hall, past the man in the suit, past the older woman, past the prostitute. He stopped in front of the kid and waited for him to look up. It took a few seconds. The kid's hair was thick, the color of dried leaves, maybe three weeks past needing a cut. He slowly sat back and raised his head to look directly into Rawls's eyes, his expression devoid of all emotion.

Rawls felt something throb deep within his gut. He had seen that expression before, on other faces. The face of a mother who had lost her only child. The face of a man who had just learned he would be spending the rest of his life in prison. The face of a girl who woke up to find that she would never walk again. A look of despair so deep and profound . . . it was as if the connections between the mind and the face were severed, leaving only a terrible blankness.

He had seen that expression in other places too. The morgue. Funeral parlors. Murder scenes.

The face of the dead.

But this boy was not dead. Somewhere behind those eyes there existed a spark—a spark that had brought him here, to this building, to this bench, to George Rawls.

"Are you Shayne?" Rawls asked.

The boy dropped his chin. Rawls took that as a yes and sat beside him on the bench, feeling every last one of his forty-three years, fifteen of them as a cop. Despite having conducted hundreds of such interviews, he found himself at a loss. Something about this kid—who could not have weighed much more than his Labrador retriever—frightened him. Not fear for himself. The other kind of fear: fear that the universe no longer made sense, that everything was about to change.

"So . . . ," Rawls cleared his throat, looking straight ahead, ". . . who did you kill?"

I met Shayne the same day I got busted for having drugs in my locker, which was also the day after this huge thunderstorm that knocked over a bunch of trees, including the giant elm in our backyard.

I was walking to school. I had left home early so I could look at the storm damage. I could hear chain saws from every direction. Each block had three or four trees down. Some had fallen on houses, some against power lines, and there was even one big oak tree completely blocking Thirty-first Street.

None of the buses had arrived yet when I got to the school. As I started up the wide, shallow steps leading to the front door I heard a humming, burbling sound and looked back to see a motorcycle pull up to the curb. A battered BMW, at least thirty years old. The tank and fenders were painted primer gray. The seat was patched with duct tape. The rider, dressed in a black T-shirt and black jeans, put down the kickstand and took off his helmet.

My first thought: *He looks too young to have a driver's license.*

He ran his fingers through his hair, hung his helmet

on the mirror, looked at me, looked at the school, looked back at me.

"Nice suit," he said. He had a soft, crisp voice, and some kind of accent.

"Thanks." I was wearing my dark gray three-button, the one with the cuffed trousers. "Nice bike," I said. I can be a little sarcastic sometimes.

He looked down at his battered motorcycle. "Not really." He gestured at the school building. "You go here?"

"Why else would I be here?"

He nodded. "Me too. I just moved here. I start today. Where's the student parking?" Definitely an accent—maybe southern, but with a sharp edge to it.

"See that sign?" I pointed. "That huge sign that says STUDENT PARKING?"

"Oh," he said.

Once again looking at my suit, he said, "Is there, like, a dress code or something?"

I took in his frayed T-shirt, his holey jeans, his beat-up black cowboy boots. "Lucky for you, no. As long as you don't wear gang colors or a T-shirt with swear words."

He nodded. "So what's with the suit?" He didn't ask it meanly, just in a mildly curious way.

"Some people like to dress nice," I said.

He nodded as if he understood, popped the helmet back on his head, turned the bike around, and rode off toward the parking lot.

I didn't even know his name, but already I liked him.

---

*Mi nombre es Miguel Martín*, and no, I am not Mexican. Actually, I am Haitian on my mom's side. Her parents came from Haiti back in 1971. They speak Haitian French. I am learning Spanish, however. My mom wanted me to learn French, but learning Spanish is more useful on account of I am often mistaken for Mexican, even by Mexicans, which is weird because Pépé—Mom's dad—is black. That deep purple-black skin color that comes from the west coast of Africa via Haiti. My grandmother, Mémé, is freckled, red-headed, and white. Her ancestors sailed to Haiti from France back in the 1600s. That's her story, anyway. These days her red hair is from a dye bottle, but she claims it's her real color.

My mom turned out to be a medium-brown-skinned woman with Afro hair that turns reddish in the summer. My dad is white, third or fourth generation Italian American.

Anyway, when all those genes got mixed up, I somehow came out looking Mexican. Imagine a Mexican kid, kind of small, wearing a suit and oversize tortoiseshell glasses. That's me. My sister, Marie—we're in the same grade even though she's ten months older than me—has light skin and our grandma's freckles, but her features are more African-looking.

My real name is Mike Martin, aka Mikey the Munchkin, and a *bueno día* is any day I don't feel the need to slink, or, in *español, escabullirse.* Do you know about slinking? It's a way of moving from place to place so people don't notice you. Cats are very good at it. Rats are even better. Lions and polar bears never slink. Okay, maybe a little, but only when they're sneaking up on you.

I have noticed that most short guys (I am the shortest guy in the eleventh grade) adopt one of two strategies. Some, like Chris Rock, or Prince, or Napoleon, have these enormous, noisy egos and make up for their lack of size by dressing and talking big. Others just try not to get stepped on. This is also true of small dogs, which tend to be either world-class barkers or world-class slinkers.

I do it all. I dress big, I bark, and I slink.

I *escabullirse*d into American Lit class and took my usual seat near the windows a few seconds before the 7:40 chime. A few minutes later, the kid with the BMW walked in. Mr. Clemens gave him a raised-eyebrow look.

"Sorry I'm late, sir," he said. "My name is Shayne. With a *Y*. Shayne Blank. I just transferred here."

Mr. Clemens, startled by all his politeness, directed Shayne-with-a-*Y* Blank to the empty desk next to me.

Here's what was weird. Every one of us had our eyes on him, the way we would stare at any new face, but this kid appeared to be perfectly comfortable, relaxed, confident, and alert. I've met cats that could pull that off—that combination of hyperalertness and megaconfidence—but I'd never seen it in a human. So, after class, being a friendly and inquisitive type of guy, I followed him into the hall and introduced myself properly. We went through the whole where-are-you-from-what-are-you-doing-here routine—he told me he was originally from Fartlick, Idaho, and that his dad was on a secret mission to Afghanistan, and that his mom was in the Witness Protection Program, and he was living with his aunt.

"I suppose she's an astronaut or something," I said.

"Yes. But from another planet."

I liked his sense of humor.

"I thought maybe you were from the South. Because of your accent."

"I have no accent," he said, in an accent.

"So is Blank your real name? Or an alias?"

He frowned. "You don't like it?"

I was opening my mouth to say something back to him when I felt a hand clamp down on my shoulder.

"Hey, Mikey."

"Hey, Jon," I said, trying to act as if I was glad to see him.

Jon Brande was borderline movie star handsome, with blond hair, sparkly blue eyes, a strong chin, and a toothpasted smile—the picture of a vibrant, healthy teenager, ready to graduate with honors, accept a basketball scholarship to a Big Ten university, and go on to enjoy a brilliant career in politics. Except that Jon had been kicked off the basketball team his sophomore year and his grades were just barely passing.

Also, he was a violent, psychotic, drug-dealing creep.

"Listen." He hung his arm around my shoulders and turned me so our backs were to Shayne. "You got room for this in your backpack?" He handed me a brown paper lunch bag. It was limp and wrinkled, as if it had been opened and closed several times. "Just hold it for me. I'll get it back from you after school."

All my alarm bells were going off, but there was no way I could refuse. Jon was big, he was a senior, and he scared the crap out of me. I took the bag. I didn't have to ask him what was in it, but I couldn't help asking, "Why?"

"No reason." He winked and walked off.

Believe me, it is very creepy to get winked at by Jon Brande.

Shayne said, "Friend of yours?"

"Not really." I stuffed the paper bag into my backpack. "He's my sister's boyfriend."

# PETE HAUTMAN

godless

PETE HAUTMAN Author of *Sweetblood*

PETE HAUTMAN

Author of SWEETBLOOD

PETE HAUTMAN

National Book Award–winning author of GODLESS

PETE HAUTMAN

National Book Award–winning author of GODLESS

PETE HAUTMAN

Author of *Godless*, the National Book Award winner

rash

PETE HAUTMAN

National Book Award–winning author of GODLESS

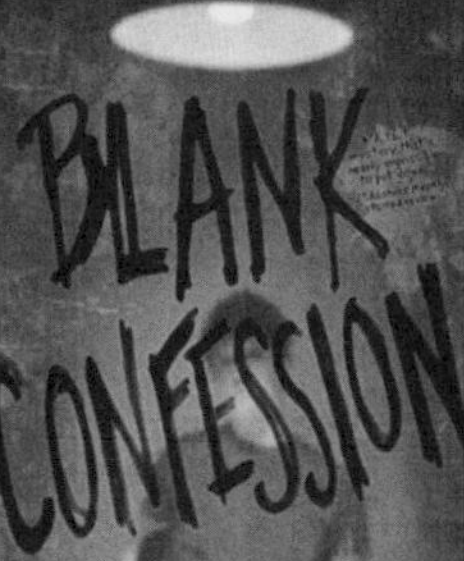


Sweetblood

PETE HAUTMAN

Author of Godless, National Book Award winner